THE KNIGHT OF
HIBERNIA

J. SCOT WITTY

To order additional copies of this book, contact:
Bookwhip
1-855-339-3589
https://www.bookwhip.com

CONTENTS

THE BEGINNING

Since the dawn of time, men of all walks of life have struggled to understand the ebbs and flows of fate as it slowly and patiently carves a path through the lives of the unsuspecting. The great builder and destroyer, fate, may cause one great misery and inspire another to strive to heights never before seen.

A man who earns a humble wage working a hole in the ground to feed his family may be fated to discover a way to turn lifeless iron into something more by the seemingly accidental means giving life to steel, the thing that men of great power desire. These accidental events could change a man's status and station in life, giving him the freedoms of an important lord of the land. It may also indenture him to an obligation to his lord, thus leaving him with fewer freedoms than a man of half his wealth or importance. Regardless of how many new freedoms a man may achieve in his new life, the freedom to live a simple life moves slowly and without warning ever further out of reach.

A woman in a mud-crusted hut struggled with all her might to bring a new life into the world. The worried faces of the women around her showed concern, for the child was coming the wrong way out. High above the hut, in the cold night sky, the moon loomed full and silent but gave no comfort, for the child inside the mother was dying. The shamaness took the hand of the woman, her face full of tears, and told her to stop, for in order to save her life, the other must falter. The woman looked deep into the eyes of the shamaness, who was adorned with her headdress made of the antler of a young stag, and began to relax. In the quiet of the night, the woman heard the thunder of wild horses running outside the hut and began to feel an overwhelming love coming from inside her—a love so pure in this world filled with darkness that it could not be denied. The mother pushed to bring her child into the world, and with her last breath, she heard the cry of a new life born into the world. A young woman took the baby and placed him in the hands of the shamaness. At a loss of what had to be done next, she looked into the eyes of this new being and knew what had to be done.

The local lord was a man buried in mediocrity as he struggled to make a better life. He was not born into nobility, but as fate weaved her tapestry, he, by an accident at the forge, had turned the iron found in the mines, which were too soft to be used for anything, into steel, the lifeblood of an empire. However, this newfound fortune did not give him comfort for illness, and loss wrought him into a harsh and cold man, unable to even speak to his only son. In the darkness of the night, he wandered the large and empty manor, haunted by the memories of the love now gone from the world. He could not sleep, for the pain he felt in his heart was sometimes too much for him to endure. Those around him judged him with spite or envy, for he never spoke of the ailments he suffered. In the welcomed silence, he stood at the window, looking out at the moon high over the land. An oddly dressed old woman was walking toward his house. She wore a dark cloak and seemed to have horns atop her head. Fearing that this might be some specter bringing evil intent to his door, he quickly ran to bolt the lock, but it was too late.

The door stood open as the dark figure stood with the light of the moon behind her. The wind ruffled her cloak as she stood hunched, holding a gnarled staff. The horns atop her head made her seem large and menacing as she waited in silence. The lord cowered and begged forgiveness for whatever he had done to bring such evil before him.

"You are the man they call LaCross," an ethereal voice emanating from somewhere within the large cloak asked, followed by a thunderclap.

The lord lifted his head to the figure, nodded, and feared what would come next.

"I come bearing a gift for your house," the shamaness said, staring into the nobleman's eyes as if to pierce his very soul. "A blessing for what shall come to pass."

The man looked away in fear as she opened her robe and removed the tattered cloth that had been protecting the infant from the cold. As the nobleman began to rise from his prone position, the shamaness deliberately placed the quiet and steady child into his ready hands.

"This is a child. What is the meaning of this?" he demanded as his arrogance gave birth to anger. He looked up at the old woman, who now seemed more like a crazy hag than a shamaness.

"I am glad you noticed that it be a child. Look into his eyes," she said with conviction. "He has an old soul, and he has been here before."

These were difficult days for everyone, but more so for LaCross. Since his accidental discovery, he had unwittingly indentured himself to the warlord who ruled over the lands of Cornwall. It was getting harder to quench the thirst for steel of the Cornish king and manage the fields for growing food as well. LaCross could feel himself instinctually passing the baby back to the old woman, but when he felt the tiny hand grab on to his finger, he looked down into the smiling face of the small nameless infant. It was as if the tiny child had known him. As he held the child, a feeling came over the coldhearted man that he had not felt in a very long time. The giant man, scared by the years of disappointment and despair, began to smile as a tear ran down his face. The fear of the night had begun to melt away as his heart began to beat once more. But who was this child, and where did it come from? The nobleman turned toward the door where the shamaness had been standing, but only the empty, cold night remained. She was gone and was never to be seen again.

He closed the heavy door and looked down into the eyes of the tiny creature and said, "You will be called Dar. Dar LaCross."

Many years later, the skinny, barefoot young Dar LaCross spent his days running in the fields with the prize horses, which were the pride of Lyonesse; climbing the high mountains; and merrymaking with the peasants who worked the land for his disapproving father. This was frowned upon, but Lord LaCross allowed it, giving his son moments of happiness that he himself envied. He grew up listening to legends of the dragons who once ruled the land and of the elves who lived in the world between worlds. However, for Dar, listening to these stories was not enough. He soon began to explore forbidden ruins and dark caves, searching for what none knew.

Soon Dar found himself poised hesitantly, having walked into a dark unfamiliar cave seeking a wise old man who the villagers had only known as Gob. When he climbed the high cliff to reach the crack in the world, he did not know what he would find. Some had said that Gob was not a real person. Dar was not afraid, and standing before him, in the dark cave where no one dared to tread, was Gob, a hermit who had not been acquainted with a bath since his quest for mushrooms and knowledge had begun. Dar offered the old man a loaf of bread, as is the custom of his people, his outstretched hand trembling.

The old man, unaccustomed to visitors, looked up at the one so young. Dar's eyes watered from the offending odor of promises broken and a life askew. The old man snatched the bread with the precision and speed of the lethal strike of a mountain lion making a meal of an unsuspecting lamb grazing happily in the fields of the river valley. The boy jumped and fell backward onto a log that only moments ago had gone unnoticed in the shadowy darkness cast by the dim firelight illuminating the face of the hermit and giving him the appearance of a devil in the darkness.

"Are you afraid, boy?" the hermit asked crassly, with bits of bread falling from his mouth. "Do you think I shall eat you?"

The boy welled all the courage he could muster and spoke softly but firmly, "I'm not afraid of you."

"Good. Why you be here, boy? Speak up, boy!" he said, pointing with a freshly mauled piece of bread.

"I have a question for you. That is what you do here, is it not? You are supposed to be the wisest of the wise—"

"A question," the hermit interrupted. "You are too young to have *ques-tions*, boy! Why don't you go home now and come back after you have lived enough to have a real question worthy of my time? You need to find a girl! Make some babies, and then when you have lived enough life, you come back to me with a real question." The man resumed mauling the bread with his broken and blackened teeth, the sight of which turned Dar's stomach.

The boy, looking very disappointed, turned away from the sight of the old man melting back into the dirt and muck from which he came. His feet, encouraged to leave the cave with some haste, failed to be motivated from the lack of instructions of the thinking engine, which engaged in an internal argument with itself. The boy was thinking about his question. This was the wise man who answered questions that were important and life-changing. He had given his life to passing wisdom from the spirit world to the mundane in order to teach people how to live a better life. The boy sharply turned to the face of the shattered soul before him, his face red from frustration as he breathed with the determination of a bull. The man's face pierced through the light of the flames as he looked up at the boy's face. Sparks from the fire framed his devilish face and reached to consume the empty space of the hollow above.

"How can a man change his destiny?" The question left the lips of the boy with such determination that it did not get entangled in the echo of the space of the cave.

The hermit lifted his head in surprise, gleaning a look of a man who, for the first time in his life, had not been disappointed by someone claiming to have an important question worthy of him to answer. "Now that," he said, "*is* a real question. What is it that you want, my boy?"

The boy began to explain using a variety of hand gestures to tell his story. "My father works all day in the dark beneath the ground to take the ore found and turn it into steel for the king. He comes home black with soot late at night. He sometimes coughs so hard that blood drips from his lips onto a kerchief, which he keeps by his bed. He was a free man before the steel, and now that he has become a noble, he is more slave than before. I would like to find another way for my father, but it would seem that we have been fated to our success."

"You wish freedom for your father but nothing for yourself, boy?" the old man asked suspiciously.

"I must find the fates, you must tell me where, and plead with them to change my father's destiny," the boy replied.

The hermit listened to the conviction of every word the poor boy spoke. He realized that the boy would not be able to save his father, for his fate had already been written. He noticed the boy's feet, red and sore from the long climb to his threshold, and wondered if the boy was strong enough to change his fate. When the boy was finished with his story, the hermit moved in close to the boy's face until they were nearly touching noses and skillfully chose words to discourage.

"These things are written in the stars, boy. They were aligned that way on the day you were born. Look up to the sky and you will see that it never changes. They remain for all times, as does your fate."

The boy stood up and shouted, "But I am willing to do whatever it takes to change them! You must tell me how!"

The old man jumped from his crouching position, enraged. "You will do anything to change the heavens itself? To reorder the stars in the sky? You are no boy! You are a demon come to torment me! You try to trick me to get me to violate the order of things and take my soul!" The old hermit tossed the bread at the boy's feet and yelled, "Be gone with you, fair demon! Be gone!"

The boy looked down at the cowering lump of dust and grime and spoke softly so as not to frighten him, "I am just a boy, not a demon. I was told that you were the wisest, but I see that you are just a tired old man who has forgotten his wits long ago. Keep the bread. I mean you no harm, old man. I will leave you now, as you wish."

The boy turned and walked from the man. As he stood at the mouth of the cave, overlooking the countryside, he readied himself to accept whatever fate had to offer him. As he looked, he could see his home of Lyonesse and remarked on how small it all looked. He looked down at his feet, bare and covered in mud, much like that of the hermit, and smiled and accepted whoever he was to become. As he lifted his foot to make his way back to the land of what was to be, a grime-covered hand grabbed his arm and turned his gaze toward the hermit once more. His appearance was different from before. The hermit stood more like a man; his eyes were wide and knowing. *This*, the boy thought, *is the look of a wise man.*

"Boy," he said, stern yet gentle, "boy, the fates sit tirelessly at their looms weaving our future for us. They arrange the stars so that we don't lose our way, but if you are strong enough to imagine a different path, yet unseen, then you may change your destiny. You will reorder your life and the lives of those you touch. Use your power wisely."

"So it is possible? It sounds easy," the boy asked, hanging on to every word.

"That it is, boy, but it comes with a price. If you change your path, then you become the architect of your own existence, thus changing the world itself. You become responsible for the lives of the people around you.

The good and the bad will become your doing. Are you strong enough for that, boy?"

Dar turned away as if in a daze from this knowledge swirling around in his head. This was surely an answer worth climbing the mountain for. But what did it mean to be responsible for the lives of the people around him? What was this magic that would change the world and the people? The boy quickly turned back to face the old hermit once more.

"But—" It was too late. Standing on the hilltop, the boy was alone.

CHAPTER 1

THE ARRIVAL

The moon hung high in the shimmering night sky, casting its light over the vast and sprawling wilderness below. Clouds, which only moments ago insisted on pelting the land with their seemingly endless raindrops, were now quietly drifting across the sky, ever so gently caressing the silver halo of glowing light reflected in the round face of the moon. It seemed that the clouds themselves somehow knew that the moon's beams of light would be guiding a change so profound that it would change everything for the beings below forever. In the darkness of the night, a tiny silhouette of a small cloaked figure stood on the endless sandy beach of Hibernia for the first time.

The relentless falling rain had finally subsided; the clouds were drifting apart and allowing more of the magical light of the moon to shine through. The mysterious figure on the beach below, in delight that he could see, took the opportunity to once again scan the coastline, hoping that the extra light would at least allow him to see something, anything indicating a city was nearby. But no matter how much he strained his eyes in the darkness, he still only saw waves lapping the coastline, with no evidence that a city had ever existed. He was beginning to realize that his long journey to find the famed knights of Hibernia, his quest to join the most beloved and coveted protectors of the people, was proving to also be a quest requiring cunning and skill that would prove he was worthy to be counted among them.

Simply thinking of the stories of the knights of Hibernia and finding them made him stand a bit taller. As he puffed out his chest with pride, a whisper came from his lips, "I can do this." He realized that his journey would surely become an expedition befitting of a true knight. It would become an adventure full of mystery and danger. But where should he find these men of Hibernia, ironclad of honor and grace? He wondered if they would find him worthy or if he would fall into obscurity.

Hidden under the deep protection of his cloak, Dar LaCross shook his head while glancing around, confusion taking over. He was certain that he had landed in the correct location, yet there was no sign of the city anywhere. This elusive city, the city of Aonoch, was not only supposed to be a bustling metropolis supporting vast markets, a modern bathhouse, and a large dock area at its epicenter of activity; it was also the home of the famous knights of Hibernia. He sought out to one day be counted among their number in the halls of heroes. Yet somehow the city was conspicuously missing from the beachhead where he stood. Scratching his head, Dar began to wonder if he had made a mistake in his calculations and landed on the wrong beach.

Dar was the leading authority—well, the only authority—on all things Hibernia. He had meticulously studied from the mysterious book that he found about the land and its people. He had learned about their kings and customs. Dar had spent months at the docks near Lyonesse talking to merchant sailors and fishermen. Dar was the first person from Cornwall to actually set foot in Hibernia in a very long time, but all the rumors matched up with what Dar had understood from his reading. He quickly dismissed the possibility of what he thought he knew had been wrong and scanned the unfamiliar landscape for a clue as to where he should go next.

Dar tilted his face toward the sky and held out his hand to determine if the rain had finally stopped falling, an age-old scientific meteorological method of discovery still in use to this day. Satisfied that it would not rain any longer, he peeled the hood from his head, revealing his youthful, boyish face. Without thinking, his hand instinctually reached into his pocket to retrieve a small square tightly wrapped in a heavy cloth, a protective covering carefully designed to keep his treasure from getting wet during the long journey across the sea. Bringing it to his other hand, he began to perform the ritual he had rehearsed many times before, gingerly loosening the twine used to hold his prize securely wrapped in the cloth. As if unaware of the motions of his hands, he unfolded the protective covering, turning it over in his hands. A smile began to spread across his face when he dislodged the book that was quite important to him from its resting place tucked within the heavy pale cloth, now drifting from his fingertips toward the floor of the small boat now resting on the beach.

Dar began to appraise the condition of the book, concerned that the seawater might have penetrated the protective shell and began to thumb through it. The pages were yellowed with time and made a crinkling sound when he opened the book. It was quite old, just how old was unknown, with a leather binding that felt soft to the touch. The oils from his fingers left imprints on the cover where his hands had held the book many times while stealing moments from his work and play to read the words that conjured images and content of the world he was preparing to explore. He admired the fading but still vibrant inked pages that would have taken hundreds of monks years to recreate if they had the inclination to do so. He ran his finger along the edge where it had been scarred and burned, giving it the appearance that a hungry nibbler had chewed it in hopes of finding nourishment from the pages within. In spite of the fact that he had given the book great care, some of the pages were loose and had released their grip on the spine that held them together. The pages, loose but not lost, were all accounted for.

Tracing his finger along the ragged edge of the corner of the cover, encircling the burn patterns, he could almost hear the voice of his father on the night he had decided to leave his home. His father, depreciating the book that had captivated his son's attentions during the last year, had thrown the cursed thing into the fire in an attempt to be rid of it forever and keep his son home, where it was safe. However, after speaking with the wise man on the hill, Dar was destined to take action that would find him on a distant shore across the sea.

The moonlight was barely enough to see by but was better than the darkness of the cloudy sky just moments before. Dar slipped his finger carefully within the ragged pages marked by a thin red cloth leaf. As he opened the book to the page, the page unfolded to reveal an intricate color inked drawing. Turning the book on its side, he viewed the likeness of the land laid out before him. In the past, Dar had spent months studying the map and admiring its details, as made by someone intimate with the untamed wilderness. With the gentle waves rocking the boat against the rocks behind him, Dar stood meticulously comparing the shoreline with the drawing for the very first time. His finger found the city of Aonoch and the mountains to the north, and he looked up at the land stretching before him. Straining his eyes against the darkness, he spotted the similar contours of the land drawn on the map.

A puzzled expression affixed itself on his face as he was able to identify every element on the beach, with the exception of the missing city. He began to wonder what purpose the map held for the person who had made it. *Why would anyone make a map with such detail and draw a city where one does not exist?* he pondered. In the margins of the map were lines accompanied with a semblance of mysterious symbols, which he assumed must have been some strange language. Dar did not understand the meaning of the lines but began to suspect that the markings must have held some esoteric meaning as to why the city was missing. He turned and looked back across the sea from where he had come in his little boat and began to feel the full gravity of his actions. Cornwall was nowhere to be seen on the horizon. Dar realized that he was committed to finding the honored knights and making a life in this new land. Returning his gaze toward the future he had chosen, Dar prepared to take his first steps onto the sandy shore of the land of Hibernia.

As he glanced up and down the empty beach, the gentle crashing of the waves under the moonlight was the only companionship found. Reaching into the bottom of the boat, Dar lifted a heavy bag out of the boat and placed it on a large rock just beneath. The bag, which contained all the belongings he thought he would need for his journey, felt moist to the touch and made a *clink* sound when it hit the surface. Dar then took his book and began to fold the map to place it back into the book where it had come from. With a single deliberate stroke, he shoved it securely into the pocket of his coat and slung the bag over his shoulder.

As Dar thought back to all the times he had studied the map in secret, stealing moments at all odd hours of the day and night, it had never occurred to Dar that the map could be wrong. After all, mapmaking was not something that people did. Even in Cornwall, there were no mapmakers. As he walked along the lonely beach, contemplating where he should go now, he looked in all directions for a sign. The night was dark, but it illuminated the contours of the hills and cliffs enough that he could see where he was going. That was when he spotted the old man hill. Dar quickly removed the map from his pocket to see if what he was seeing was real. The map showed various details of items that were used as a sort of landmark. Painted on the map in the location of the beach where he was standing was what Dar had always thought was a rock in the shape of an old man kneeling, but as he stood with the map in hand, Dar traced the contour of the hill face, which matched the drawing perfectly. The kneeling old man was the hill facing the sea. This was it. The map was right, and he was in the right place. He contemplated for a moment that if this detail of the map was correct, then often things might also be correct and he just had to find the real city of the knights.

Armed with new hope, Dar observed that there was a path from the beachhead leading up through the old man hill on the map. Above the hill, through the woods, were small villages that dotted the countryside. Dar realized that if he could find the path to the highlands, he could find one of these villages and then find the city of the knights. Dar took the cloth previously used to protect his book and began to wrap the book once more. After using the twine to secure it, he took his bag from his shoulder and pushed the book to the bottom of the bag, where it would be safe with all his gear. He took an oil lantern from the bag and fastened it to the outside of the bag. He was unsure of what would happen to him, but he was sure that whatever bounty his destiny would bring, he was prepared for it.

Strange and colorful birds that had been roosting in a nearby tree were watching silently as the two-legged creature, unfamiliar to these shores, readjusted the hood of his cloak to cover his head and began to walk along the beach toward them. As Dar fumbled his way, his footing unsteady on the slippery rocks wet from the recent rain and the spray of the sea disturbed the silence of the night with a sudden explosion of birds from the trees that grew from the cliff that fortified the beach. Dar paused for a moment, his clothes still wet from the rain, as a shiver ran through his body. He lifted his clothes away from his body in an attempt to feel more comfortable, with hopes that they would soon dry out. Realizing that his heavy clothes would make it difficult to climb the cliff if it would come to that, he considered finding a place to make a fire and get dry. With his bag bouncing from left to right over his shoulder, Dar made his way to the incline where the map had shown the path leading up to the highland. It was dark, but Dar could just make out an overhang along the cliff, where he could make a fire and keep out of the elements should it decide to rain again.

Dar had never traveled so far from home before and was unaccustomed to the ways of navigating the unfamiliar terrain, and out of the excitement of finally starting his adventure, he began to run toward the ridge. The rocks peppering the sandy coastline were slippery from a thin coating of algae, which drew its nourishment from what the tide would bring in on a regular basis. Running, Dar attempted some semblance of grace but managed to slip and fall on the rocks, landing hard on one and banging his head on another. From his newfound prone position, he lifted his head to see that the overlook was not that far from where he had fallen. He slowly rose to his feet and pined for the warmth of the fire that he would build and walked the rest of the way.

Reaching the cliff face, Dar stood staring up at the side of the cliff that met the beach. A sudden feeling of apprehension overtook him, as the cliff was much steeper than it had seemed from the edge of the water. He began to look around for some dry wood with which to make a fire. The driftwood was sufficiently dried out and bleached from the sun as he collected pieces that seemed dry enough to catch fire. Wandering around the beach and collecting wood, Dar continued to glance at the high cliff that he would have to scale in the morning. He hoped it would look easier when the sun was lighting his way.

Suddenly a loud howl pierced the night, giving Dar such a fright that he slipped on a rock and dropped the wood he had been carrying. After picking himself up off the sand once more, he reminded himself that a risky climb in the dark probably gave him a better chance at survival than staying overnight on the beach and taking the risk of needing to fight off any large hungry creatures that might see a tasty morsel camping alone and that might make a delicious meal of him. After considering all the mysterious creatures his imagination manufactured in those few moments, the cliff did not seem so treacherous after all. He decided to make the climb under the cover of darkness.

Leaving the pile of collected wood behind, Dar searched for the promised path that would lead him to the top of the cliff. As he looked through the scrub that grew on a gradual incline, the path was not readily visible from the shadow cast by the cliff blocking the moonlight. Dar made his way onto the incline, which was more a pile of large boulders covered with a thick overgrown brush than a path, and with the exhilaration of finally beginning his quest, he began to make his way to the top. He was thrilled that he might be able to make it all the way to the top of the summit of the cliff in the dark without suffering any further injuries. Dar climbed with confidence while keeping his eyes on the sky to be alerted to any swooping creatures that might be living in this strange land.

Dar managed to climb roughly halfway to the top of the cliff relatively easily by leaping from one boulder to the next. Being quite pleased with himself, he reached a group of large pointy rocks that seemed to jut out from the cliff face, which he was using as a midway point marker. He decided to sit and rest before going any farther. He was getting tired and did not want to lose his footing and fall to the bottom. It was an ideal spot to sit and rest without fear of losing his footing. After situating himself on one of the large rocks protruding from the great wall, with his gear beside him, he took the opportunity to stand and look around in order to gain more of a comprehensive take of the landscape and better appraisal of his situation. He looked back down at the bottom from where he had climbed and then up at the amount of rock he had yet to climb.

Observing that the steep incline above was made up of loose rocks and plants growing from the cliff wall, he realized that the remaining climb was going to be more challenging without his climbing equipment. He needed a grappling hook. While praising himself for being the type of person who was always prepared for any eventuality, such as this, he reached deep into his bag in order to rummage through his gear for the rope. He remembered that he had placed the hook right next to the rope so he would remember to tie them together when he had packed. Feeling around in the dark, he found the rope and began to pull it from its place among the menagerie of equipment Dar had packed. He beamed with pride as he pulled the rope into view, but the smile suddenly faded when he reached the end of his rope and found no hook attached. He bit his lip as he rummaged through the bag once more for the hook, but he did not find it. A loud sigh escaped his lips as the realization that he had forgotten it set in.

Feeling that the rope would be useless, he used it to tie his bag in a way that he could loop it over his shoulders and fit it squarely on the small of his back. Tugging it one way and then the next, he centered it tightly on his back. Giving himself a silent pep talk, he gained the courage to continue his climb. He leaned out of the safety of the rock shelf he had been sitting on and reached and grabbed a stone and pulled himself up and onto the cliff wall. Holding on, he moved his foot back and forth, looking for a solid place to put his feet. As he reached up again, the hood fell from his head and rested on his shoulders atop his pack. The light from the moon set his pale skin aglow, making it easier to see as he began to climb the steep incline to the top. Luckily, he thought to himself, no one was watching the spectacle he was making of the climb, as he was too scared to look down at his feet and was too afraid of falling to let go as he pressed his body against the wall, shifting back and forth, much like a large bat scaling a flat wall.

Mud and sand began to accumulate within the gaps of his fingers, which were still wet from the recent rains. Often he imagined himself on such an adventure, blazing new trails where men dare not travel and sailing to distant shores; he even imagined climbing cliffs and mountains to rescue fair maidens in distress, but he never imagined the cold, slimy reality that he now faced. A slimy film of sand, mud, and grass gathered in the front of his shirt and down his trousers from the overhang above. Hoping to get out of the river of sludge, Dar reached to his far left and felt around for a place to grab on to. Holding on, his body shifted in a natural way, leaving his right foot to drift off the rock. Suddenly, his left foot slipped from the rock it was resting on, and Dar was left dangling from one hand. As his body twisted, the fingers of his left hand tightened its grip, for fear of dropping to the bottom. Dar struggled to gain his composure and to reach the wall with his right hand. Frantically twisting his body, he felt around with his free hand until he found a root that had grown out from the ground, and he grabbed on to bring his body close to the cliff wall.

His feet hanging in the air, Dar looked down along his body to find some place to put his feet. A sick feeling came over him when he saw how high off the ground he was. The reality of falling began to set in when his body, exhausted from the climb, went limp. He knew that he just had to continue. He was too close to reaching his goal to give up. He began to dig his foot into the cliff wall, making a divot in which he could place his foot.

Once anchored, he lifted his other foot, bringing his knee to his chest, in order to place it on another root. Satisfied that it would hold his weight, Dar reached up to find another handhold to lift himself up. The muscles in his arm burned and felt as if they would jump right out of his body. As he reached up, a large rock fell from its resting place and hit his shoulder on the way down; he cursed himself for forgetting the grappling hook.

Reaching up once more, he found he had finally reached the top of the overhang. A barrier of dirt and grass roots stood between him and victory. Dar took his hand and began drilling a hole through the soft mud. His fingers reached the top, and he could finally feel the grass that grew atop the cliff. Reaching almost to the sky, Dar grabbed a tiny bit of earth, but he could not force his way through to the top. He made sure his feet were anchored on the roots where he stood, and he took his other hand, tracking it up his arm through the mud of the overhang, and began to make the hole larger. Moving his arms back and forth, he was able to see the sky through the earth barrier.

A howl escaped Dar's lungs as sharp pains sprang from his arms and legs as the young man struggled to pull himself up through the bottom of the ledge by his fingers. The unnatural sound got the attention of a large elk that was grazing near the forest edge. It watched as some premarital creature rose from the earth, as if willing itself into existence from the earth itself, and then the proud elk ran off in panic. Covered in mud, Dar attempted to wipe the mud from his face, but his hands, also mud-covered, could only remove the mound of mud caked around his eyes. Bright blinking eyes appeared on the dark mud figure that was Dar. He howled in pain once more. Now sore from head to toe, feeling pain in places he never knew could hurt, Dar collapsed onto the cool grass to rest from his ordeal.

The cool grass was soothing to his aching body as he quietly waited for the unfamiliar pains to subside. Lying on his back, unable to move, he looked to the stars in the sky above. Dar had often looked up at the stars and noticed that it seemed to be the same stars he had always admired from his home so far away. His breath deepened, for he now knew that he was not alone on his quest. The lights in the sky represented the windows of his ancestors, and he knew that the spirits of the past were watching him, judging him for what he was doing and would do. He smiled as he imagined what they would say to him after climbing the wall. Perhaps they would say, "Don't do it, it's dangerous." He watched the clouds move across the sky as they released the moon into view. The sky was clear enough that the rabbit shadow began to appear on the face of the moon.

"What are you looking at? This is all your fault!" he yelled, as if it could somehow hear him. He began to relax and fell into a dream.

Dar LaCross was the youngest son of one of the earls of Cornwall, the land across the sea. He was all of thirteen, and by Cornish standards, he was a man. This gave him many freedoms, but it also came with many responsibilities. Although he was an obedient son, he resisted many things that were expected of him. His father, being a self-made noble only by the whims of the king, knew that his sons would not inherit his titles and would end up indentured to whomever the king would give the mines to; he began introducing Dar and his older brother, Ambrose, to the noblewomen of the five kingdoms to marry.

He knew that arranging marriages for his sons would have to be a careful endeavor, for his sons, although they had many prospects, did not have titles. Many noblewomen, wanting to meet Dar for his reputation, would travel far and wide. He was a kind and gentle soul, with a strong sense of honor that made many a noble father interested in bringing him into their company. His older brother, Ambrose, was a bit harder to match, for his reputation also traveled far and wide. Unlike his brother Dar, Ambrose had always known he would grow into a life of privilege and grace. This made him an uncouth braggart who enjoyed drinking ale and spreading untruths about people and himself just a little too much. He spent much of his time in the company of soldiers and picked up their detached way of looking at things. This left many of the noblewomen of Britain cold and uninterested. However, because of Dar's handsome features and his unusual straw-colored hair, the women who were invited to meet Ambrose only came for the opportunity to meet the younger brother, infuriating Ambrose even more.

Throughout the five kingdoms, it was unusual for a man considered even a lesser noble to work alongside the lowborn, but Dar did just that. He enjoyed the work and had a knack for it. Rumors circulated throughout Lyonesse and eventually into Cornwall itself that Dar would often help some of the elderly and sick workers by chopping wood for them in the middle of the night or fixing the thatch on their rooftops to keep the rain from coming in. Dar even brought meat for those who could not hunt for it. The lowborn of Lyonesse loved and respected Dar for what he did for them, and hearing of this would make Ambrose sick.

Ambrose worked to tarnish Dar's reputation while spreading stories about him to the people gathered in the pubs, but they would not take. In the evenings, Ambrose would often find his brother trading stories around the campfire in the center of the village where the workers lived. He would tell them stories of things that the craftsmen and traders who came to visit the earl to sell their wares would tell, and they would look to him like he was some kind of saint. Standing in the shadows of his brother, Ambrose knew that he had to find a way to discredit Dar before he would inherit everything that Ambrose had considered his.

Overall, life was good in Lyonesse. The earl was not a heavy-handed noble like the Cornish nobles had been in the past, and he had put less demands on the lowborn people living on his land. As long as the iron flowed from the mines, the earl allowed the common folk to live as they chose and by their old traditions. For the earl, iron was his paramount concern, for it was what made the earl an earl in the first place, for he was once a lowborn like them. Knowing this gave the common folk a feeling of pride to know that their landlord understood their situation and exercised the power to change it. The earl gave the common folk dignity that translated into strong loyalty and hard work ethic, which made the earl very prosperous in the kingdom but in turn also made him one of the most hated by other nobles.

One day in the early spring, Dar was laughing with the mine workers as their workday ended. It had felt good to get into the warm sun even though the frost-covered grass still crunched under their feet. A fire was waiting for them to warm themselves with while the women of the village would serve them the meal of the day. Dar warmed his hands while the wives of his fellow workers catered to their needs. He thought it would be nice to find someone who loved him as much as the lowborn women loved their husbands. For Dar, love was not in the equation, for he would be matched with a noblewoman who found his wealth attractive, not his character. As he daydreamed, a young woman from the village, who had eyes for Dar but realized long ago that the attention he might give to her, a common woman, might become hazardous to her health, handed him a bowl of something he could not identify. He held his hand up as if to deny her of something precious.

"You have to eat! It's not much, but it is what we have," she urged while rolling her eyes.

As he stretched out his arm to take the bowl, he was bumped by an older man who was out of breath and panting. In his excitement, he bounced from one leg to the other, frantically pointing while he struggled to say something. Dar set down his bowl, which was mostly empty as the contents were dripping down his leg, and tried to calm the man enough to speak. He thought, *What could make the man so upset?*

"Is there fire in the village?" he inquired, glancing in the direction the man was pointing. Dar did not see smoke, so there was obviously no fire.

The man grabbed a canteen from the outstretched hand of one of the workers and took a long, rapid drink. With water dripping down his face and neck, the man lowered the canteen and uttered one word that filled the brave and hardy mine workers with terror.

"Dragon! There!"

Wide-eyed and with great haste, Dar left the man and grabbed his coat, which had been resting on the tree stump where he had left it hours ago. He ran to the edge of the clearing, where a lone buckskin horse stood happily chewing grass in the enclosure where Dar had left her earlier that morning. When he opened the gate to the paddock, she lifted her head and trotted over to him in anticipation of going home. Dar placed the harness over her head and nose, attaching it firmly in place, and whispered in her ear. They would not be going home today, for there was a dragon approaching the village. The horse, as if the words were understood, lifted her head, grunted, and nodded in acceptance.

As if rehearsed, Dar leaped onto the back of the horse in a single smooth motion and trotted out of the opened gate. He guided her over to the section of the fence where a small shed stood holding an accordion of spears, each with a unique steel blade on its tip. After Dar lifted one from its holder and tested it in his hand, they, horse and rider, took off like a shot from a cannon and bolted down the hillside toward the direction the frightened man had pointed. Dar was not afraid of dragons because they were not much more than a nuisance most of the time. They meant no real harm and were more afraid of humans than expected of a creature of its size.

The Cornish dragons were curious creatures indeed, not at all like the famous winged dragons of Cambria, which had died off centuries ago. The Cornish dragons were large wingless lizards that typically weighed up to seven hundred pounds. In spite of being wingless, at six feet in length, they had a tail that could snap a man in half given the opportunity. They would crawl up from the lowlands of Lyonesse in search of an otherwise useless white stone, which formed when the waters of the storm season, midsummer, would recede and dry on the surface. No one knew what they used the stones for, but without fail, they would come and dig it out wherever it might have formed. In the early summer, the villagers would dig out the stones and drag them to the lowlands, which kept the dragons from coming up to the village in search of them. But this was not midsummer, when the dragons searched for the stone, which meant that this dragon was either sick or hungry. Either way, it also meant that it was very dangerous.

With lightning speed, Dar rocketed toward the village. As Dar knew that he might have to fight the giant beast, his stomach dropped, causing him to clinch his legs together around the mare's midriff, signaling for her to run faster yet. The hooves of his horse roared over the small bridge, which crossed the gorge below. She was more forward than he was used to, and he pulled back on the reins when the dragon came into view. The head of the mare yanked Dar to the side, and she stopped moving closer to the dragon. Dar stroked her neck to calm her down and to prepare for the difficult task ahead. He directed the horse to slowly move toward the great beast, but she would not have it. She stood like a statue frozen in place, refusing to move. Dar scratched her head and reached down to rub her face. He whispered in her ear once more, and the horse seemed ready to go on, nodding in agreement.

The dragon was larger than any Dar had ever seen. The dark skin was stained with yellow markings that ran down its length and showed its vast age. Dragons this old had never been seen before; there was no account of how it would react, but Dar had to try to frighten it off just the same. Dar angled the point of the spear toward the dragon in case it decided to lunge at him as he encircled the beast on the horse. This was a well-known tactic, which was designed to make the dragon dizzy so it would return to its home in the lowlands. Without warning, the beast swiped its massive claw at the passing spear and sliced through it like a hot knife through butter. Dar tossed the spear aside and continued to encircle the dragon faster, hoping that it would get tired of this game and go home.

The dragon twisted and turned to keep up with Dar, but he was too fast for him. He spit at Dar's horse with its corrosive poison, the beast's main offensive weapon, to immobilize him, but no matter how hard it tried, Dar kept his horse away from the beast's mouth. In the dragon's arsenal was a second enzyme that, on rare occasions, it would spit out—a sticky black oil-like substance that would ignite, burning anything and everything it touched. Even water could burn in the wake of a dragon attack of this type. This allowed a cunning dragon to make a hasty escape while the humans were busy dealing with other things.

Having had an interest in dragons, Dar learned as much as he could from the wise men who wandered the countryside. In his studies, he had discovered that the great beast had a small soft patch of flesh on the side of its head in which it would hear from. This was its Achilles' heel—a weakness, uncovered by the hard, bony armor of its skin, which, if struck hard enough, even with a blunt spear, could stop the beast in its tracks. Dar respected all creatures large and small and tried very hard not to kill an animal unless he was hunting for food or unless it was unavoidable. Dar hoped this would not be one of those times.

Barreling around toward the dragon's head, Dar scanned for an opening to strike the creature in its soft spot. As his horse passed in front of the beast, the dragon snapped its large body and lunged at the passing horse. As the dragon grabbed the horse with its talons, the horse reared up and kicked the monster with her hooves. Kicking to get the beast to let go of her, she reared up again and knocked the dragon on its head. Having lost all control of his horse, Dar struggled to hold on to her reins, but when she bucked, he rolled off her shoulder and landed hard on the ground, having the wind knocked out of him. With lightning reflexes, the enormous beast grated Dar's horse with its giant claws, throwing the steed to the ground. She quickly rolled over and got up to move away from the creature. Bucking and spitting, the horse protested, leaving Dar to the beast.

Lying flat on his back and covered with blood, Dar scrambled to find his spear, knowing that the dragon would soon be on him. Spotting the spear, he moved to grab it, but the large creature had grabbed the torn leg of his trouser and began pulling him closer. Dar could not reach the spear. Spinning around, Dar kicked the dragon and quickly began moving away, crawling like a crab, but the beast was soon upon him. Dar grabbed the beast by its throat and forcibly pushed the large snapping jaws away from his face while reaching frantically for his spear. As the spear was blunted and now broken, Dar could not believe his luck as the great beast struggled to eat him. With all his might, Dar began to stab the beast repeatedly in the throat with the fragment of his spear, but it was to no avail. As the beast opened its jaws to deliver the attack it had hoped would be the end of this fierce struggle, Dar shoved the spear's remnant into its mouth, piercing the roof of the monster's mouth.

The beast curled and cowered in pain caused by the annoying human. Dar began to wiggle out from beneath the heavy claws of the great beast to try to escape, but the sheer weight of the creature had him pinned. It turned on Dar once more to deliver its final blow, which would end the struggle and allow it to eat, when a rather strange-looking large rabbit, seemingly unaware of the quarrel in its midst, leaped in front of Dar, getting the dragon's attention away from him. The dragon, stunned by the fearless creature, snapped at the rabbit as it leaped across its snout. The dragon, obsessed with this new and much easier prey to deal with, kicked Dar away and perused the rabbit across the field, away from the village.

Many who had seen the gaping claw marks on Dar's horse had spotted the dragon making its way across the fields. Soon there was an outcry that Dar LaCross, the son of the earl, had been devoured by the dragon. For the men of the mine, this was an outrage that could not go unavenged. Walking toward the village with their pickaxes and other assorted work implements, the angry men found the offending dragon eating what they imagined in their minds was their beloved Dar. They immediately began yelling at the beast to both scare the creature and alert other men to their location. As the dragon met this new threat, it began to spit and coil to gain a vantage point to strike the shouting mob with its tail. Fearing what the dragon might do, for they were not dragon hunters, the men began to dance around the great beast, just as they had seen Dar do many times before. Swinging their axes at the beast, one or two of them thumped the animal on the tail and head as they moved around it.

The people of the entire village were soon rushing into the fields toward the yelling men. Breaking off from the mob, a little girl had noticed something strange and was curious to see what it was. Her attention was consumed by what she had thought was her pet cat sitting at the edge of the chasm, but as she moved closer, the animal had somehow become a large rabbit and hopped down the embankment. Confused, she followed where the rabbit was going with her eyes, for she had been told many times that it was dangerous. As she peered over the edge, she spotted the seemingly lifeless body of Dar lying at the bottom. Excited by the fact that he had not been eaten, she ran to the edge of the field and began yelling for her father.

"Papa, come quick! Dar is over there," she screamed and pointed over the embankment. "He is alive!"

The men of the village turned to the direction of the little girl to hear her words clearer. The dragon noticed that the attention of angry humans wielding heavy pointed tools designed the crack hard stones was no longer centered on it and thought that this might be a good time to flee the scene and return to its home, where it could enjoy an easier supper. The men began to run toward the little girl when the dragon began to lumber off as fast as its short legs could take him. Soon the dragon was gone, and the people rejoiced that the village had not been burned by a dragon attack.

Dar awoke hearing the voices of the villagers as they carefully made their way down the steep climb to the bottom of the gorge. One of the larger men had looped a rope around a nearby rock and began to lower the rope while holding it in place. One by one, the mine workers began to climb down to rescue their beloved lord. To his surprise, although Dar found it difficult to breathe, he found himself alive. He imagined what kind of damage the creature had inflicted on him and shuddered. He remarked that he was not in as much pain as he would have expected and tried to get to his feet.

"I am all right," he said, raising an arm. "I just need to get to my feet."

Dar did not get to his feet. He leaned to one side and lifted his head but found it to be too much for him and fell to his shoulder after losing his composure. He found it very painful to move at all, lying with his head partially in the water. He turned over once again and saw the looks of the concerned men moving toward him. As the world began to fade and turn white, he noticed the rabbit sitting on a rock, staring at him.

"You! Thank you, sir," Dar said to the rabbit.

In his delirium, the rabbit seemed to smile and wink at him as he drifted in and out of lucidness. By the time the large men were gingerly lifting his body to get him up the embankment, Dar was slipping into obscurity, when he began shouting and pointing to the rabbit they could not see. The men brought Dar to his feet and held him in place just as he requested, but they could still not see the rabbit in question that had been taunting him in his delirium.

One of the men began to doubt his eyes and cautiously crept over to where Dar was seeing the elusive rabbit. He looked around but could not find any sign of a rabbit; however, he did see a strange-looking bundle of clothing tucked in with some of the larger stones. His curiosity gained the attention of another man who had walked over and insisted on helping with the discovery. The new man picked up a stick and started poking at what they had found. As the cloth moved, it uncovered the body of a man, decayed for a year or more. The men began to collect the remains of the man, whom they might have known. Dar watched with careful concentration, when a face appeared, filling his sight.

"Don't worry! We goin' to git ya ta da surgeon straightaway," the face assured him as he passed into unconsciousness.

After a time, recovering from his blow, Dar found himself in the bed of the surgeon who had done a remarkable job of sewing up his wounds and dousing him with herbs and dun. The smell was enough to wake the dead, and now he was certain that he wasn't. With his nose full of the smell, his eyes began to water and his vision began to clear. Sitting on the table in front of him was a large leather bag. It was an unusual bag that looked as if it had been made for a special purpose. It had belonged to the body that the villagers had found in the ravine, and although the community was very small, they could not identify the remains. They simply buried the body and returned his bag to the only person the villagers knew could find who he was. And there the bag sat, waiting for Dar to uncover its secrets.

Dar pulled the bag toward him and began to untie the drawstrings that held the flap in place, keeping its contents safe from the elements. As he opened the flap, images of what treasures he would find inside began to fill his imagination. The bag was empty. Dar dragged the bag closer to him and tilted it to reach his arm inside. Reaching in deep, Dar felt something with his fingertips, but it was lodged at the bottom. He put the bag between his knees to get a good grip on it, and then, with both hands, he yanked at the thing at the bottom. After he pulled it back and forth, it came loose. It was a book. Dar's eyes widened as he opened it. It was all handwritten with great care. No one in Cornwall had ever seen a book, and Dar imagined this must be very important.

For a man of Cornwall, a book was a treasure indeed. When Dar opened the cover of the mysterious book, it had a musty smell from having been in the river so long. The pages were dry and made a crinkling noise when he turned them. The cover was made of leather, with the pages stitched in to form a codex. It was written in a language he had never seen before; there were drawings throughout the book, which held very little meaning to Dar. Also hidden in the bag were four flat metal rings that appeared to have once been attached to one another in some fashion. He had hoped that the book might give the secrets of this item and the man whom it all had belonged to.

Once Dar had recovered and was ready to leave the home of the surgeon, he took the strange book home with him for further study. After a time, Dar found that there were many things he did not understand about the book. When walking began to get easier for him, Dar took the book to the wise man whom he became friends with many years before. The old man studied the book carefully. The old man had been a child when he had last seen a book, and to hold one in his hand brought him back to a simpler time.

"Back then they," he remarked, "were all written in the imperial language, but this isn't one of those. This book seems to be written mostly in Hibernian and something I have not seen before. It must have been written there. Do you know of Hibernia? It lies across the sea beyond the fog. I can teach you how to read the Hibernian parts for a chicken." The old man smiled through broken teeth and spit in his hand and held it out.

"Wait a minute, isn't Hibernia a wilderness? I mean, nobody really lives there, do they?" Dar asked, repeating information he had heard from a traveling trader.

The old man slapped the boy on the forehead. "You can't say nobody lives there till you been there, boy."

After holding the book in his hands and hearing the story of the rabbit, the old man had realized that the strange book was a part of Dar's destiny in some way. The book was a codex of detailed information about Hibernia and its people. It had several quires of stories that the sage found indicative of an older culture. They told of a sage king who ruled Hibernia. Dar gravitated to tales that told of a group of knights that roamed the countryside, helping the lowborn people and keeping the peace between the nobles. Farmers and traders alike were protected by the knights of Hibernia from the jealous and selfish lords, giving them rights akin to those of the gentry. Hearing these tales gave Dar a sense of pride and purpose.

In the many weeks that followed, the LaCross chicken house began to suffer slow and steady loses. Dar spent hours stealing time away from his work and sleep while he read the many heroic adventures that made up the quire.

Now lying in the grass on the distant shore of the land that possessed his every waking thought, he decided to rest and find his bearings when the sun rose. Dar sat comfortably on the grass as he opened his bag and reached to the bottom to retrieve the prized book that he carried within. After fumbling around the contents, he soon dislodged the book from its resting place. The book, still wrapped carefully, was covered with silt from the difficult climb. Dar took the side of his hand and scrapped the mud off the sides and wiped it on his pants. Fearful that it might have gotten wet, he began to unwind the protective cloth slowly. He was pleased to discover that the mud had been confined to the outer layer of the cloth and did not permeate through to the book.

Dar slowly took everything out of his bag and inspected all the contents. While his rope was wet and muddy, it was still useful, and he wound it in a neat coil and strapped it to his belt. In order to be a knight, Dar made some metal bits, which he designed based on the descriptions he had read of the armor belonging to the knights. A set of greaves were clear of mud, and he strapped them to his shins to protect his legs and knees. A large round, flat hammered piece of steel was secured back into the pack, for fear that it would be too hard for him to get through the forest that lay ahead of him. He shoved his book deep in the empty void of his pocket, where he knew it would be safe, and then settled down for a nap.

CHAPTER 2

ᴛʜᴇ Pʀɪᴄᴇ Oғ Pᴇᴀᴄᴇ

It had been thirty years since the iron men of the then-fledgling empire of Caledonia had invaded and swept through the Marche in an attempt to conquer all of Hibernia. Although the invasion did give the Caledonian king a strong foothold in what they called Dál Araide and in other areas along the coast, they failed to occupy the far regions of Hibernia. But the people of Hibernia would not have such men conquer them. Cities like Providence and Gateway remained independent and important ports throughout the region and provided resistance from their influence.

After suffering great losses on the battlefield, the conqueror Aviticus of Caledonia devised a different strategy. The main stronghold was an ancient city called Eamhain. He had realized that, to solidify his power in the region, he had to control this ancient kingdom. Ruled by a sorceress, the city was awe-inspiring to the great conqueror and his men. With its great walls, a defense built to protect its people from a larger army a century ago, the city would prove to be impervious to Aviticus's army. He had decided that his only option was to build large catapults and bombard the city with fiery pitch in the night while they slept and annihilate the threat.

His plan had worked. The once-great city was reduced to a flaming ruin before the armies of Hibernia could be mobilized. Moreover, at the moment of his great victory, just when the fortress of the grand city was about to be breached, ensuring a swift victory, the armies of Aviticus had gone away. Confused, the surviving leaders of Eamhain had sent out scouts to determine their fate, but they could not find any armies, only one man. Aviticus had left his most-trusted general, Iohannes Mandor, to broker the peace.

Although the sorceress, leader of the city, was killed in the onslaught, her consort met with General Mandor. He explained that Aviticus did not want him to surrender the city but instead wanted him to continue to rule but give his loyalty to Aviticus. The consort scoffed at the thought and attempted to arrest the lone general. The unarmed general then went on to explain that, during the night, they had rounded up many of the cities' children, who were trying to flee the fire.

"They will be educated and well taken care of. That is, as long as we can count on your support in this region," he explained with great guile.

Having no real choice, the consort agreed and became duke of the Marche, which is what Aviticus renamed the ancient kingdom. Feeling betrayed, the other warring clans continued to attack the Marche and the military outpost along the shoreline, to no avail. The invaders were in Hibernia to stay, and the people of Hibernia retreated into the hills, where Aviticus's soldiers would not follow. However, there would be no peace for Aviticus and his followers. For thirty years, they struggled to maintain their borders against the relentless attacks of the Hibernian tribes trying to take back their land; but eventually, the people forgot how the war began, and the fighting ended. The people of the Marche were lost and afraid without the sorceress, but soon it was time for Lady Ysbeth, daughter of the sorceress and her consort, to return to the kingdom of her mother and rule as duchess of the Marche.

In spite of being appointed by the Marche's shadow leader, Aviticus, Lady Ysbeth of Eamhain returned to her rightful lands while many of the noble leaders throughout the Marche felt that the position should have gone to one of them. But she was a true noble, and as she toured through the territory, she took the time to meet with all the lowborn folk, to discover despair among them unsurpassed. She began to visit with the black monks who her mother had relayed for various inventions that they would create. The black monks, so named for the stains on their hands and faces caused by the ink they used for their writings of scientific study, soon developed machines that would help the common people in their labors; but not everyone was happy with these new developments.

In just a few weeks, the duchess, Lady Ysbeth, had reorganized the business in the Marche to benefit all who lived there. In the wake of Aviticus's control of the area, her father had set up a system where the noble counts would collect the taxes for Aviticus's men. For the most part, this meant that the counts had control over the welfare of the people for which they ruled, but in reality, the counts had set up a system where they ensured their own prosperity, leaving those who worked their life away for the Marche to be fated to live in poverty. To better control the work they did, the counts had developed the method of control over the people by setting up farming communities in which the people would no longer own their farm and would have to get permission from their count to move to another area. But when Duchess Ysbeth came to the Marche, she began to change all that.

The care and concern that Lady Ysbeth showed for the common folk infuriated the nobles under her charge. They believed she was helping Aviticus dilute their control over the people, but in reality, it was she who was exerting control over the counts. Over time, the noble counts began to meet in secret to organize a coup against this new duchess. The counts began to meet in ill-lit halls in the middle of the night to discuss the steps they would take to maintain their wealth and control. Among the conspirators was Lord Bennu, a young count who did not know just how things were supposed to work in the kingdom. He felt that the counts should go to the duchess herself and persuade her to give up her current trappings and prepare for war against Aviticus.

The young count was a tall yet very thin man who seemed to have legs that were disproportionate to the rest of his body. Having recently been selected to the position by the unfortunate acts of banditry performed by the previous count, he was ill-educated and unprepared for the job expected of him. Aware of his shortcomings, he listened to the way the other counts spoke and, in an attempt to sound qualified, emulated how they spoke. He was count of one of the largest territories in the Marche. The other counts felt that they needed him on their side. However, after many meetings, Lord Bennu did not like the treasonous sound of the meetings and decided to speak with the duchess herself.

As he had recently been a member of the peasantry, old habits were hard to break; the count made a long ride on the back of an ass to the castle of the duchess, and on the long journey, he considered all the things he would discuss with her. There were Aviticus's tax collectors, who always seemed to take more than their share; his army, which also took supplies whenever they came across his lands; and the conditions in which this had left his people. But more importantly, he wanted her to know that in spite of that, he was not raiding his fellow count's lands, as his predecessor did, and he still maintained an army with which to liberate the people of the Marche when she was ready. He rehearsed over and over while traveling through the length of the Marche and wrapped it all in a language that would make him sound educated so that she would take his announcement with a grain of seriousness.

As he was standing in the center of the large room, in front of so many people, tradesmen, farmers, and his coconspirators, the words that filled his head began to evaporate in a moment of terror. He began attempting to explain his presence without acknowledging the plot against her. After an hour of rambling and using words he did not know the meaning of while waving his hands wildly in the air to give the appearance of importance, the young count stood quietly in a silent room, waiting for the duchess to respond. The room was filled with a menagerie of awestruck faces contemplating some point that everyone had missed. Fayette, one of the duchess's ladies whose job it was to assist Ysbeth in all matters and to sometimes interpret the ramblings of an idiot, recognized the expression of wonder. She quietly brought a tray with a goblet of water to the duchess and leaned in to whisper so that only she could hear.

"He has raised an army and wants to war against Aviticus to liberate the Marche." As the words left her lips, like magic, the duchess seemed to spring to life in an animated fashion.

"You do not seem to understand our situation here, my lord"— Fayette whispered his name for her while she struggled to remember— "Lord Bennu, you represent one town, be it a larger farming and trade center, but it is a limited population all the same. How can we expect to hold our own against the largest army Hibernia has ever known? The truth is that we are all subjects to the whims of Aviticus. He has the right to take what he wants and do as he pleases. In a war against him, the people, whom you claim to be here to protect, will be the ones who will suffer. I have to consider the welfare of all the people I am responsible for. You see, I have been to the Baile. I have seen his army. His people are not like us. They are ruthless professional soldiers who will raise every town, every village, if we attempt to rise against him."

"Mum, you are adequately peregrinating the dangerous situation in which your attendants have inclined themselves to," the count said, fumbling his words.

Fayette began to lean in toward the duchess but was stopped when she lifted her hand and began to speak with a stern look on her face, "It is not time for such actions. I understand you all too well, my lord Bennu, and I trust that you will acquiesce to the wisdom of my advisers."

The room was once again silent as the duchess took another sip of water from the goblet being held by Fayette. It had been a long day, and she looked tired. She gave a subtle and well-rehearsed gesture to the chamberlain, who, in attendance, would stand just behind the sitting sovereign with a sword at the ready. He abruptly announced that court was adjourned for the day. As the people all began to leave the hallowed room, the young count stood motionless, looking very cross as he watched the duchess and her lady leave the room. His face was red with anger, and his eyebrows formed an eleven on his head while his hand instinctively caressed the pommel of his sword. Aware of the moment, the chamberlain quickly moved between the count and the duchess, but as he, too, began to turn to leave the room, the count moved up and grabbed his arm.

"Sir, I am unsatisfied! I demand that you admit me to speak with her exaltedness again. My eternal eagerness to conversate the furtive information of the magnanimous counts to whom I am speaking forthwith," the count said with an air of expectation.

The chamberlain picked up the count's hand to remove from his arm by lifting it with two fingers, as if removing the rotten carcass of some dead rodent that had been left on his doorstep.

"That will not be possible. Court has been adjourned. You may make a special request to speak further with her if you choose," the chamberlain advised. "The duchess has heard your important message, and I assure you, my lord, that you will be rewarded for your efforts accordingly. I will make a certain effort that the duchess does not forget you. Now please return to your country home, and soon you will hear from us."

The chamberlain left the young man standing in the empty room as the castle staff began to extinguish the lamps illuminating the hall. Shaking his head, the chamberlain entered the antechamber of the duchess. Without a word, he walked over to a small table to the side of the room and washed his hands. Grabbing a towel to dry himself, he turned to Lady Ysbeth, who was smiling at the strange ritual. Fayette was helping the duchess out of an elegant dress that somehow seemed better fitting for a woman twice her size, held together by a broach so as not to appear ill-fitting. As the chamberlain gazed at her, he noted that the dress was a reminder of a more civilized time, when a sorceress had ruled over the land many years before.

"You wear that dress as beautifully as your mother ever did," he said with a voice that might bring a tear, but the chamberlain rarely showed any emotion and never shed a tear.

The chamberlain could only be described as ancient, although he was very spry for a man of his advanced age. In addition to taking care of the dukedom's finances, he also served as the thegn, commanding the duchess's armies and personal guard. Although no one knew just how long the chamberlain had served in Eamhain, it was said that he had outlived everyone who had known him as younger. Sickly thin, his wrinkled face and hands were a testament of his many years, but he seemed to have an uncanny strength and never seemed to tire. He always spoke in a calm, level manner almost fluid in sound, which gave Lady Ysbeth comfort. His steady demeanor surrounded him, accompanied by a sickening, sweet floral smell of the liniment he would douse himself with, claiming that it was the key to his youthful looks. Fayette had noted that he never looked into a mirror.

"I hope you took in what he was saying out there," said the duchess. "Maybe we should send him a gift of allegiance in a couple of days? I mean to say—"

"The man is an idiot! Why entertain any ideas around this man at all?" The chamberlain was flippant.

"The man brought to you knowledge of growing discontent among the gentry that has been organizing right under your nose," she stated calmly. "As Fayette reminded me, he is also the largest landowner among the noble lords. If we can get him on our side, it would quell any opposing addendums to keeping the peace until an opportunity presents itself to do otherwise."

"So what sort of gift do you have in mind?" the chamberlain asked innocently, shifting his stance to follow the duchess into the private courtyard.

"I was thinking of a marriage proposal," she blurted out, bouncing across the grass toward the inner keep in her flowing white undergarments.

The chamberlain cracked a smile that looked quite reptilian in nature and said, "Marriage! I imagine his youth could be appealing, but isn't he a bit below your station to be considering—"

"Not me, you fool," Ysbeth interrupted. She looked at him crossly but half smiling as she chose her words carefully to explain, "Here in the keep, we have all the young ladies who were either orphaned or lost their lands and titles to young men like this Count Bennu. What better way to reinstate them into the gentry where they belong than through legitimate marriages with the current gentry, whom we do not trust? This will demonstrate to the counts that I want to support their claims by legitimizing their positions. Gain their loyalty, and we get eyes and ears in their houses."

"In addition to the royal ladies embedded throughout the gentry at the ears of the counts, you will end up having direct control of their lands, indirectly. It's brilliant!" the chamberlain said, elated.

The duchess stopped walking for a moment and turned to look into his emotionless face. "Leave it to you to turn an innocent arrangement into something else. You are more devious than I have given you credit for, but I see your point. Look to your scrolls and make an appropriate selection. I will talk to them."

The chamberlain agreed with the plan and stalked away to write a letter to the count and to start making preparations for the arrangement. Meanwhile, the duchess smiled at Fayette, who was patiently waiting.

"You know all the ladies living here. Why, they are like sisters to you. Who would you choose to marry the young Count Bennu of Teamhrach?"

Fayette scrunched her face while she thought for a moment, and then, like a light, she had an idea. "I think Lady Mahj should marry him. She is the daughter of the old high king. It will be good for her because the people of Teamhrach know of her and will follow her. The count will say,

'Oh, the daughter of the high king, how nice.' He will feel you have given him importance, and he will give you his loyalty. Meanwhile, Lady Mahj will be your eyes and ears in the largest county."

The duchess was pleased with her thoughtfulness and agreed, "Let's talk to Mahj, and then we can make the announcement."

In the months that followed, the duchess and the count of Teamhrach corresponded frequently, with great progress toward making the wedding arrangements. It was to be a simple affair, with little fanfare. The duchess convinced him that this would reduce the jealous acts that might come his way from the other counts. This was more for Mahj's safety than for his, but knowing and having met the other counts in secret, he believed this to be true. Having been impressed with his initiative to train soldiers, the duchess assured him that after the wedding, he would be given a more appropriate position in her court as master at arms. This would put him in a position to raise and train an army that the duchess would command.

During this time, without the count of Teamhrach, the conspiracy to replace the duchess began to lose mobility. The secret meetings where the counts met in a dark secret room began getting smaller each passing day. It seemed that the rumbling of thunder that had rolled throughout the noble houses of the gentry had blown over, and the gray skies of discord had cleared, giving way to the bright sunny days where a noble wedding was brewing. And soon came the day for the count to finally meet his bride-to-be.

On the ancient cobble road where for centuries the kings of old would make their pilgrimage, barefoot as one who has nothing, to the high hilltop where the great stone enclosure lay, the place where the mother of all came to venture into the underworld to save her children, to marry the great high priestess to become high king, a rickety wagon had been slowly rumbling for what seemed like an age to its occupants.

As the midday sun stood high over the rolling green hills, the heat from the wagon began to cook the ladies riding within. Growing weary of the heat of the long journey, Fayette stood on the soft pillows and the thick blankets spread across the floor of the wagon in an attempt to make the trip bearable. By now convinced that the pillows were filled with rocks, she tried to maintain her balance as she made her way to the front of the box, where a small window was located. She carefully slid back a small panel and leaned in to enjoy the airflow.

On the other side of the window, two soldiers sat at the reins, driving the heavy wagon. She leaned in, shoving her face through the small opening, to speak with the driver. As she opened her mouth to speak, a moment of ecstasy whisked her voice away, leaving only the cool breeze of the open air caressing her face and neck.

The guard sitting next to the driver had noticed her and asked, "Didja want somtin', ma'lady?"

"We both are very hot and tired. Can we find a place to stop and rest awhile?" Fayette asked, enjoying another moment of air.

"We be comin' ta da clearin' at da reservoir just ahead, ma'lady.

We kin you can rest awile there," the man answered.

Fayette thanked the young man and slid the window closed again but left it cracked open just enough to let some cool air into the cabin. The two weary women stared at each other as the men continued talking, unaware that there were women listening. As the conversation went to places where women will always find offense, Fayette and Mahj simply laughed out loud as the wagon lurched back and forth in the worn ruts of the road. Mahj braced herself, for fear that the cabin would come apart. Fayette assured her that it would hold together, and the two women laughed again as the wagon lurched to a stop.

In the clearing, a herd of elk were grazing on the grass along the embankment of the reservoir. A red-horned buck lifted his head to see what was causing the rumbling noise as the wagon arrived at the far end of the pond. When the humans disembarked from the loud box, the buck let out a howl to warn other creatures that two-leggers were coming and then guided the herd into the forest. Two soldiers armed with only a sword at their side, designed to protect the ladies from other humans who might, at any moment, become foes, stepped off the large platform mounted in the rear of the wagon. On the alert, they quickly scanned the area to ascertain the origin of the strange and horrifying sound. Dedicated to their duty, the two men began thrusting their swords into the nearby bushes to uncover a few birds hiding from the foul-smelling creatures.

As the birds flew away from the area, the two soldiers returned to the wagon, signaling to the third soldier, who was riding atop the wagon, that all was safe. The youngest of the three soldiers had returned his sword to its sheath and hopped down from the wagon to let his passengers out to stretch their legs. His chest filled with pride, for he was the youngest to be given such an honor, as he began to unlatch the rear panel of the wagon. When the door swung open, the smile on the young soldier's face soon melted away to escape the wretched smell that smacked him in the face, leaving only a blank expression. The two ladies had been forced to sweat for hours while they traveled across the Marche to where they would finally feel the relief of the grass under their feet.

The interior of the wagon was made to seem luxurious for the long journey, and they had almost gotten everything right. Silks were draped along the walls to hide the sharp edges of the roof and soften the interior of the cabin, which was a little more than a prison on wheels. Along the floor were two mattresses filled with down. Having handled chicken, ducks, and geese, the thought of a down feather mattress had sounded like the ideal in luxury travel to Fayette, but her rump was not agreeing. By the time the wagon had stopped to give the two ladies a break from the oven in which they rode, the mattresses felt like they were filled with rocks, and the ladies were thrilled to get off them for a few moments.

After the young soldier had recovered from the lingering odor, he crawled inside the wagon and opened all the small windows and propped the main door open. He hoped this would remove offense to his senses. In the years that followed, he would often relate this event with great enthusiasm but would describe the smell as that of a skunk that had crawled into the cabin to die and had been undiscovered for many months. Nevertheless, in spite of this, the smiles of Mahj and Fayette when he opened the main door would forever be etched into his memory.

Mahj was a tall slender woman who towered over most men who lived in the castle. The ringlets of her long golden hair bounced as she walked from the wagon to rub her toes into the grass. With her hair shining in the sun, the fair skin of her funny face and the sparkle of her eyes, blue as the petals of the small and rare deep-blue flowers that grow and carpet the fields of her homeland, gave her a stunning appearance, which made many living in the Marche consider her the most beautiful woman in the world. In spite of this and her noble heritage, she had had no suitors, for a woman without a dowry also had no prospects, and that was stolen from her during the Great War, which subjugated the Marche. Until recently, when the duchess had bargained for the release of the hostages of the old nobility, she had only known the life of a prisoner, but now, thanks to the duchess, she was free and was hopeful about the marriage that awaited her.

Digging her toes in the grass, she reached up to the sky as far as she could and gave out a soft moan as her back, aching from the rocking of the wagon along the bumpy road, cracked with relief. Unaware of the men who were watching her with enthrallment, she was glad to finally be out of the sweatbox that had held her captive for most of the long day's travel. She began to feel more like herself again as she looked up to notice the soldiers' gaze captured by her allure. She had always imagined that this day would come, but now that it was here, she was very uneasy about meeting the count, her future husband. She hoped that her heart would find the man and that they would share a love unmeasured, but she worried about a loveless marriage, which she would not be able to bear. She was glad the duchess had sent Fayette to travel with her.

Fayette, who had been traveling with her all day, gathered no attention and slipped away to put her feet into the cool water. She was, once again, not amused by the attention gathered about her best friend and not to her. She was tired of living in the shadow of Mahj. She often remarked that she did not understand the allure. Her bubbly disposition made the boys of the castle fall to their knees, and Fayette had always been jealous of the ability. For Fayette, most people who looked at her saw the power of the duchess, for she was always in attendance when the duchess would make her appearances. This inspired awe and fear among most, but she and Mahj were close, almost like sisters. She often wondered if this relationship would become her undoing, but for now, she reeled in the splendor of Mahj's fortuitous virtue.

Fayette had always lived in the castle with the duchess, even before the child hostages were released into her care, but she also had no dowry. Unlike the others, Fayette had no pedigree. The duchess had explained to her that her parents were not part of the old nobility and that she alone would be choosing her suitor when the time was right. When she asked for more details about her parents, the duchess always simply told her it was best that she not think about such things, for the war was an evil time, and quickly changed the subject. With no prospects of her own, Fayette had been resolved to help Mahj understand how it was done.

"What you're telling me is that my father, who was the greatest warrior of his clan, walked the King's Road barefoot from Providence, where he lived, to my mother's ancestral home of Teamhrach. He then, on his knees, pledged his life to my mother at the standing stone and then gave up everything to live with her. This is how it has always been done? So why am I to travel to the count's home of Teamhrach to marry him?" Mahj had struggled to understand the concept of a marriage to a person she had never met.

Fayette had twisted her face, as she often did when she was struggling to explain something she did not find logical. "In all fairness, the city of Teamhrach is your ancestral home, so in a sense, he would be—and is—living on your lands."

With a bit of reasoning, Mahj had begun to settle into the idea, but she was glad that Fayette would be joining her on the journey. Fayette was not overjoyed to see her sister go away from her, but she had hopes that it would all work out in the end. However, unbeknownst to either of the women, this partnership was more or less a means to an end for the duchess. Moreover, it was her scheming that brought Fayette to this place dressed in boy's clothing to conceal her appearance and her identity.

Kneeling on the bank of the lake, Fayette ran her fingers through her hair to get the tangles of the journey out. She was glad to be wearing trousers, as her hands were beginning to feel the chill of the moist air. Taking a cloth from around her neck, she dipped it into the water, catching a look of her reflection. With her hair matted with fat and wearing strange clothing, she hardly recognized herself. After ringing the water out of the cloth, she washed the sweat and dust collected from inside the wagon off her arms. The cool water felt soothing, and she began to feel better about the trip in general.

Exhausted from the wagon ride, she began to habitually unbraid her hair. This act of braiding and unbraiding her hair often put her mind at ease and made it easy to work things out in her head, but today the plans of the duchess were the only thoughts filling her mind. On the day prior to her leaving the castle, the duchess went to Fayette with the real reason for her to be traveling with Mahj to Teamhrach.

"I have had these clothes made for you especially for the trip. They will allow you to accompany Mahj without being noticed. The count will think you to be a serving boy with Mahj's retinue and won't give you a second look. This will allow you to wander his town and home unnoticed. I want you to snoop around and find out what he has been planning. You will need to find out how many soldiers he has within the walls of his town. Also, we need to find out who his coconspirators are and to make certain that he has given up on their ideals."

Fayette shifted to one foot as she let out an exasperated breath. "I thought I was going to support Mahj? I am not a spy. Isn't there someone else better suited for what you are asking? Besides, he knows what I look like. He saw me when he came to court."

The duchess tilted her head and brushed a hand against Fayette's innocent face. "Honey, I would never put you in harm's way. If the count thinks you are a serving boy, he won't actually look at you, and he won't recognize you. I want you to look around and tell me what you have seen when you return, and if you do get into trouble there, the guards I am sending have instructions to arrest you in my name to keep you safe and return you here. See, you have nothing to worry about."

They will keep you safe. In the course of her life, she had heard these words from the duchess many times. She wondered why the duchess was always concerned with keeping her safe—she, with no connections to titles or lands, a woman with no prospects. Surely, Mahj would need to be kept safe far more than she did, but it was she who the soldiers would put their lives on the line to keep safe and to return home. She often wondered if there was more to her past than the duchess ever let on, but it was never spoken of. It was true the duchess showed special affection for her, but mostly that was because she spent most of her time with her. She hoped that by helping the duchess with all things, one day she would confide in her and tell her who she was; but for now, she had to be happy with who she was.

With her feet dangling, Fayette was deep in her thoughts, when suddenly the spell was broken by the sound of Mahj calling for her. She dipped the cloth into the water once more and tossed it over her shoulder. Kneeling forward, she cupped some water in her hands to bring it to Mahj and carefully stood up so as not to lose a single drop. The guards were on the alert and seemed relieved when they saw Fayette walking up from the lake. She smiled when she saw Mahj sitting on the grass.

"Ya mustn't disappear like that, miss. We gots our orders," the older soldier said, taking her arm to drive his message home. Fayette looked into the man's face and saw the tinge of fear moving from it and continued to move toward Mahj.

"We thought you got lost," Mahj joked while smiling.

"Not today," Fayette retorted. "I brought you some water. It will cool you down."

Mahj looked at Fayette's cupped hands as she knelt down and offered the water to her. She wished she had a cup. She slowly leaned in, putting her head under Fayette's cupped hands, and drank the cool water from her fingertips. Her eyes rolled back as the water began to trickle down her neck. The two ladies had always been very close, and in spite of being younger, Fayette had always filled a motherly role in caring for her. Fayette sat down behind Mahj and cradled her head on her lap as she began to wipe her brow and face with the cloth damp from the soothing water. Mahj's body went limp under Fayette's caressing touch as she dabbed the cloth along her collarbone.

After a few moments of blissful rhapsody, Mahj sat up to let Fayette arrange her hair by grating her fingers through it as she attempted to get the knots from the long ride out. Fayette had always thought that Mahj's golden hair was beautiful, and she sang as the fair strands harmonized as they slipped off her fingers like water. Fayette then gently lowered Mahj's head to the soft grass and took the cloth from her breast and began to wash Mahj's feet and ankles.

Suddenly, like a crack of thunder, Mahj's eyes widened, and she jumped up to notice the gaze of the three guards enchanted by the two women's activities. Adjusting her dress, she announced that it was surely time they get going to finish their journey before nightfall. The wagon sank as the younger of the guards helped them back into the cabin. The door closed behind them, and the two ladies remained quiet as they listened to the clicking of the latch designed to keep them safe.

With a lurch of the wagon, they were on their way. Mahj sat very still and silent, while Fayette fought a rather difficult blanket for an attempt at comfort. Mahj watched Fayette wage bitter combat with the linens, regurgitating a cascade of undignified words. Mahj had never heard such language and was surprised that they seemed to flow from Fayette's lips so freely. As she seemed to be fighting for her life, Fayette looked up and noticed that Mahj had been staring at her with a look of worry on her face.

"Don't worry, sis, I won't be speaking in mixed company once we get to the town. I am dressed as a commoner after all," she said with a   reassuring smile while striking a pose to show her less-than-stylish clothing.

"Huh? Oh, I don't care about that." Mahj's gaze seemed to be very far away. "How long do you think you may stay with me?"

"Lady Ysbeth only wanted me to stay until you were settled into your new home," Fayette said, noticing the pouty look Mahj always had when she was not getting something she wanted. "I guess I could stay until after the wedding. Would you like that?"

Fayette had noted that, for someone who was destined to rule, Mahj was not very assertive. She and Mahj had always been very close, and having been exposed to various members of the nobility through the duchess, she had schooled her on what was expected of her. Right now they were heading to a town where everyone said it was her birthright to marry a man she had never met. Having never been in the company of a man, Mahj had no idea what to expect once she got there, and she was terrified. The fact that Fayette had seemed apprehensive about the wedding just made Mahj all the more anxious.

Mahj picked at the mattress with her finger, as if climbing into the down filling would lead her to a magical place where she would never become a countess of the Marche and she could just be a normal person, whatever that was. Fayette knew by the look on Mahj's face that if she did not say something soon, she would run away as fast as she could the moment the door to the cabin opened. This was how Mahj had dealt with uncomfortable situations throughout their lives together. The day she told Mahj about her marriage arrangement, Fayette found her hidden in the forearms of the great tree outside the castle walls.

Fayette leaned over to caress Mahj's shoulder. "You're my sister. If you want me to stay with you, I will stay as long as you need me. I will stand by you and hold your hand if you need me. Soon you will be the countess of Teamhrach, the largest of all the territories in the Marche. You will be surrounded by people who love you because your parents were kind to them. You may even one day become the duchess of the Marche. Just relax and do your thing. Everyone will love you. Nobody will question you, not even your husband."

"But, Fayette, what if he doesn't like me? Has anyone thought of that?" she whined.

Fayette began to laugh out loud at the thought that this was what she was worried about. Tears began to well up in Mahj's eyes as her lower lip began to quiver, a trait that drove Fayette absolutely mad. As teens, when anyone upset Mahj, Fayette would often be found shaking her fist at whatever demons brought tears to Mahj's eyes, and now watching the display of unbridled emotions getting the best of her, all Fayette could do was take her in her arms and wish she could have found someone else to marry the count.

Fayette took her hand, looked into the sobbing woman's eyes, and with all her heart, lied, "This is a good man. A kind and gentle man. Lady Ysbeth would not have you marry him if he wasn't. Besides, if he doesn't like you, you can always come home." She gazed into the beautiful face of Mahj and stroked her hair. She snickered ever so slightly and said, "He will like you for sure, my sweet. That, I know for certain."

Looking into the loving face of Fayette, Mahj gave her a hug and held on to her for an extra few moments than what was comfortable for two friends to do. Fayette lay next to her, cradling her in her arms, and held Mahj's hand. The two women consoled each other for the remainder of the trip, unable to see where they were going, while others decided their fate.

Sentries atop the wall that surrounded Teamhrach called for the sergeant of the guard. A portly man in an ill-fitted uniform, left over from another time, wearing a patch over one eye where he had been struck many years before, stood up from his chair, where he had been sitting most of the day. He put on his coat and grabbed his cane and began to climb the unsteady stair to the platform above the gate. The young guard, inexperienced in all things, pointed toward a lone wagon approaching on the old King's Road. The old man smiled while stroking his gray striped beard as he watched the wagon for a moment.

"Are we expecting visitors?" the old guard asked, toying with the young one.

The young guard was at a loss for words and just stared at the old man with a blank expression on his face. He then looked back at the wagon and then returned his gaze to the old guard, as if searching for an answer written in the lines of his face.

The old guard smiled and shook his head. "Ah, you don't know. You should always make sure you know who is expected when on duty at the gate. What if there were a hundred hostile soldiers hiding in that wagon? What then?" The young man looked at the wagon once more while the old guard chuckled in a way that made his coat sway from side to side.

The old man reached into his pocket and retrieved a small tin cylinder. As he held it up to his remaining eye and extended it to arm's length, the wagon came into view. He offered the tube for the young soldier to see through.

"Now what do you see?" the old guard asked.

"I see a black unmarked wagon with a driver and one guard riding on top. Oh, there is a banner." Moving the cylinder ever so slightly, the soldier was able to spot the banner of the duchess of the Marche. Like magic, he sprang to life and called to the gatekeeper to open the gates. Dread filled him as his imagination invented a scenario where he had not realized someone of such importance would be in a wagon having to wait at the great doors to the town.

The old guard collapsed the tube into a small tin circle the size of several coins rolled together and replaced it in the vest pocket of his coat. As he turned toward the stair, a smile appeared across his face as he decided to toy with the young soldier once more and paused.

"Would you like to meet the lady?" he asked.

The young soldier dropped his lance at the thought. "No, sir. Ah, thank you, sir." The young man turned toward the approaching wagon and resumed his duties.

The great doors of the town opened as the wagon careened into a space reserved for the daily deliveries of cargo and chattel needed for the general survival of the town, and the wagon lurched to a firm stop. Hearing the commotion caused by the guards and then the sound of the rattling wagon, the count emerged from the manor house, which also served as the main enclave of the town. The young count became very excited when he saw the flags on the wagon, signifying that this was the expected delivery of his bride-to-be. The courtyard was alive with activity as the guards began lining up in two rows to greet whoever was traveling in such luxury and style.

The count had a bounce in his step as he walked up to the clearing, where he was greeted by two soldiers who had been riding on the back of the wagon. The assembling men of the town were finally lined up in attention, with their lances erect in military fashion. The wagon guard saluted the count with respect to his title and presented a scroll confirming their orders. The count stood staring at the guard, who was waiting for the count to take the scroll from his hand.

"Get on with it," the count said impatiently, rolling his eyes without taking the scroll.

The soldier looked very surprised by the noble gesturing wildly at him and then ran to the rear of the wagon. The youngest of the three guards was already starting to unlatch the large rear door of the wagon, for it had been his honor. Impatient to see his bride, the count pushed the guard out of the way, knocking him to the ground, and proceeded to open the large door himself. The count's face went red with embarrassment when the opening door revealed first a pair of long slender legs belonging to the golden-haired beauty he was anxious to find. The young count had never actually seen one of these wagons before and had not known what to expect when he flung the door asunder.

Mahj was ready to leave the cabin but had to hike up her skirt to disembark the ill-designed vehicle. She was expecting the assistance of one of her escorts to help her and straighten her skirt before presenting her to the count, but she did not expect the roaming eye of the count himself. She was horrified to see the face of the count looking very much like a hungry dog waiting for his meal.

"Aaach!" Mahj screeched in the count's face when the door flew open. "Sir, you are supposed to wait over there for me." She was frantically shaking her head and pointing to the front of the wagon while she scolded him.

"Um...yes. Um...I didn't know. I...um...am sorry. I was happy to see you," the count stammered in the strange language young men often speak when a beautiful woman first speaks to them.

Remembering all the pleasantries Fayette had taught her for when she should first meet her husband-to-be, Mahj ignored them and placed a hand on his chest to ever so slightly push him aside, allowing her to unfold her legs and emerge from the wagon. Watching as she unfolded before him, mesmerized, he began to crane his neck as she continued to get taller than he had ever imagined. Towering over the young count, she turned to Fayette, who looked very much like a small sprite-faced boy, and gestured for her to disembark from the wagon and help her with her dress.

Fayette pulled the ends of Mahj's dress to straighten the creases and brushed the dust off while a moment of silence loomed over the courtyard. As if entranced by some enchantment, the count remained motionless while observing this strange ritual. The old guard, who had been slowly walking across the compound, nudged the count's arm to hand him a folded cloth and proceeded to announce the guests.

"Presenting Lady Mahj, daughter of the late Queen Ailienne of Manapii," he yelled for all to hear and then kneeled, signaling for the entire squad to follow.

Daggers darted from the eyes of the count when he turned to face the old sergeant to thank him. The count then dropped to his knee and extended his hand, less graceful than he had practiced, and waited. Mahj had been a prisoner since she had been a child and was not accustomed to such attention. Even in the home of the duchess, such rituals were few, and she was unprepared for knowing how to act. She instinctively moved to help the poor old soldier to his feet, leaving the count's hand to hover in the air. Fayette grabbed her arm, urging her to stand her ground in the silent language that women used to communicate when in the presence of men. Panic-stricken, Mahj turned to Fayette for guidance, who was gesturing for her to take the count's hand. Somehow the message did not translate, and Mahj then extended her own hand toward the count. Fayette could not believe when she saw the two dueling greeters standing erect, waiting for the other to move first. Placing her hands on Mahj's waist from behind, she slowly moved her closer to the count until their hands touched.

Stunned by her beauty and sheer height, the count attempted to talk, "Um...ah...did not realize that you would be arriving today. Not that I ain't glad to see you. I am. Glad to see you. I mean, I am glad you are here now. I would have planned something. I mean, I did plan something for your arrival. Something very special, but..." The count sighed, and in that moment, Fayette actually felt sorry for the young man. She hoped he would keep it simple, and then, while he was staring at his feet, he said, "Welcome to Teamhrach, my lady."

"You need not make a fuss, my lord. The duchess had thought it best that I come sooner than to wait until the fall," Mahj said in a soft, sincere manner.

"You must be hungry after your long journey. I have planned a great feast in your honor." This was the first of many lies that would soon ooze effortlessly from the mouth of the count before the sun set on the horizon. "I will have my servant take you to your room, where you can freshen up before the feast."

"Thank you, my lord, but I thought you did not know that I would be arriving today? How could you have planned a feast?" Mahj asked innocently.

When the words left Mahj's lips and reached Fayette's ears, she could not believe she would say such a thing. It was one thing for the young count to speak an untruth to impress her, but to call him a liar to his face was quite another. Fayette shook her head while they began walking toward the manor house.

"Oh, I planned something for you," the count lied as he looked away while he thought. "There is a goose. Yeah, a goose has been roasting all day. Since this morning. You will like it. I have the best cooks in the whole territory. And farms. I have thirty farms that deliver fresh foods every day to the town. Oh, you will like it here."

In the moments they made their way across the courtyard, Fayette observed the town, as the duchess had asked. The town was more a fort than a town. It was surrounded by a high wall made from the trunks of elder trees she imagined must have been plentiful until they were cleared to make way for the town. Small buildings were scattered around the courtyard made of stone that seemed to have been built long ago for the people whose families had always lived in Teamhrach. It seemed to Fayette that they were now the caretakers of the town. New wooden construction was found in every direction within the wall, not excluding the wall itself. All in all, the entire town looked like a work in progress to Fayette, as she thought that the duchess probably had nothing to worry about.

Mahj's eyes were beginning to water as intense boredom began taking over her brain as she listened to the count drone on about how important he was. Mahj did not much care about such things. She was used to a simple way of living and was realizing that things were about to change in her life. As her brain began to melt down, she became desperate to change the subject and stopped walking for a moment and grabbed the count's arm. "A goose dinner, you say? I guess I am hungry after all. Listen, my lord, as nice as it is to hear of your many nice things, I should really get into a bath and make myself ready for dinner." Mahj turned to Fayette and continued, "Would you help me, dear?"

Fayette was impressed with the verbal acrobatics the count was undertaking but could tell that he was annoyed at the direction Mahj had taken the conversation. Nevertheless, Mahj was taken by the elegance of the manor house itself. Resting on the edge of the courtyard, the house stood as a mockery to those living around it. It was made of heavy wood construction of which Fayette had never before witnessed. Throughout the eves along the roofline were faces and figures carved right into the structure. As they made their way up the large wooden stairs to the heavy oak double doors, Fayette noticed the odd way the older buildings were almost touching this newer manor house. It looked more like the centerpiece of some elaborate stage than a planned town.

Mahj and the count slowly walked up the graduated stair to the doors, which were held open by a man wearing a carpenter's overalls. Fayette and two of the escorts carrying a large wooden chest filled with as much clothes and shoes as Mahj could shove inside and still close the lid. The count thanked the overalled man as he went inside. The count then made a show of holding the door for Mahj to enter and then closed the door on Fayette. Bewildered, Fayette and the two soldiers stood there exchanging glances with one another, not knowing what to do next. After a few moments, the door flung open again.

"Are you coming?" Mahj asked, leaning out of the door to urge Fayette to join her. "Er, I will need my things."

Fayette rolled her eyes and entered the door behind Mahj, followed by the soldiers carrying the chest. As they entered the building, Fayette was stunned by the elegance of the interior of the house. Elaborate carvings embossed the dark wood surfaces of every archway. Visible large beams that supported the ceiling were spread every ten feet and were shaped to give the appearance of rounded walls. The centerpiece of the room was a large wooden staircase that appeared to have been carved from a single tree trunk. Its complex design with its use of dark and light wood gave the manor an elegance that Mahj and Fayette had never before seen.

Mahj and Fayette were so taken by the appearance of the room that they had not noticed the presence of the couple standing next to the large staircase, poised to serve their new guests.

"This is Doris and Clive Fulcrum. Doris runs the manor, so if you should need anything or have any problems with the staff, just let her know. Her husband, Clive, is the captain of the guard and the chief carpenter. He actually built this house. They both live here in the manor, right down the hall there, if you need them," the count explained while pointing down the hall. "If you continue down the hall there, the kitchen is at the end. Doris, would you please see Lady Mahj to her room and find a place for the young lad? Clive can show the soldiers to the barracks when they have completed their tasks."

Without a word, Doris moved to the stairs but stopped when Mahj held out her hand to greet her. Doris smiled and looked around the room at the onlookers, curtsied, and continued to the stairs to guide Mahj to her room.

"This way, mum," Doris said in a deep voice unbecoming of a woman. She stood on the stairs and waited for Mahj to follow, but Mahj had been fidgeting and craning around the room. Doris grabbed Mahj's hand and ushered her up the stairs and showed her to her room. "This is the room the young master has chosen for you. I hope it is to your liking. Should you need anything, I am just downstairs."

Doris pulled down the bedspread and checked the linens to her satisfaction. However, when she checked the large fireplace, she furrowed her eyebrows and said, "You will be needing some wood, mum. I will have my husband bring some up for ya. It can get a might bit chilly in the night here, mum. If it pleases you, the boy can come downstairs to the kitchen when he is finished getting you settled in, and Clive can find a place for 'em." Doris closed the door softly as she left the room with the soldiers who had carried Mahj's chest of clothing in.

"This house is amazing!" Mahj exclaimed with enthusiasm as she delighted in her new home while Fayette began to unpack Mahj's clothing.

Doris was only too happy that a new countess was in the house. The young master did not always eat, leaving him to grow thin and frail, and Doris was very concerned about him. She imagined he would sit for dinners on a regular basis now that a woman was here, and she was pleased with the new development. The woman's boy was a different matter. Doris felt there was something wrong with the young man but could not quite put her finger on it. She decided she would keep an eye on that one until he leaves the town.

Mahj's room was lavishly decorated and, by the looks of it, by someone who had ideas about what they thought a noblewoman would like without actually knowing one. The room was decorated in pink and trimmed with white lace. In the center of the room was a large wooden bed made from the heavy dark wood that everything else was made with; white lace looped from post to post. Against one wall was an intractably woven tapestry depicting a young soldier pledging his love for a beautiful young maiden after having killed a giant dragon, which was lying in the background. Pink curtains adorned the windows, and a large mirror stood in the corner of the room.

After looking around the room, Fayette and Mahj simply stared at each other until they broke down in laughter.

"Hey, I will no doubt be staying in the woodshed, so don't complain. I am sure you and Doris could change it up if you want," Fayette said with a snicker in her voice. "At least you know that he was thinking about you."

Mahj sat on the edge of the bed and considered her situation. Fayette sat down next to her and took her hand. Fayette thought of words she could say to make Mahj feel better, but it was Mahj who turned to Fayette and said in a soft, childlike voice, "You're right, he was thinking about me when he set up this hideous room. I think it will give me nightmares. I kinda wish someone would come along and burn it all down so I could return home with you." Mahj lay down on the soft bed and stared at the ceiling. "You know, in all the excitement, he didn't even tell me his name? Fayette, I don't even know my husband's name! What am I going to do?"

Fayette lay down on the bed next to Mahj and admired the room around them. "His name is Elli Bennu, and he is a good man. He will be a good husband for you, but the first thing we are going to do is to change this room."

Life in the kitchen of the manor was relatively easy. The count had a taste for eating cured meat and fermented foods. He also enjoyed fried foods, like potato slices and breaded chicken bits. The young count did not see the point of a dinner because he always dined alone. He got into the habit of snacking all day, passing through the kitchen when he got hungry. Demands on the cooks were relatively small, and Miles Stonecutter, the head cook, liked it that way.

Like most successful cooks, Miles was a large, fat man who loved to cook but tended to eat more than he served. Each night he would prepare a meal for the count, and each night the count would take the meat portions, tuck it between two pieces of bread, and head out the door, sending the rest back to the kitchen for the staff to eat. The result of this was that no one in the town went hungry. There was plenty of food for everyone and most of the poor, and the count liked it that way. For all his shortfalls, he hated to see people suffer.

In the middle of the kitchen was a large, heavy table, which was originally built to support the heavy lumber that Clive had built the manor. Now it served as the kitchen table, where all the nourishment of the day would be prepared. On this occasion, the table was filled with baskets of cherries gathered from the farm just outside the town walls by Miles's daughter, the small but charming Isabel. In a predominate place at the table, she sat on a high stool, where she was sampling the cherries. Miles had often thought about sending his young daughter to the duchess, where she could learn something other than kitchen work, but she seemed happy to help her father gather and prepare the food of the day. In many ways, she was more proficient than her father even was.

"Papa, what do you plan to do with all these cherries?" she asked with anticipation while helping herself to the sweet goodness.

"While you were out this morning, I made some dough, and now we can make pies with what you have brought," he answered while methodically removing the pits from each cherry with a small knife that he kept in his apron.

The small girl smiled. "The young sir should like that. He has been very sad lately. Do you suppose this will make him happy?"

"Does it make you happy?" he asked.

"Very much so." She shoveled a finger full of freshly whipped cream into her mouth.

Everyone in the manor was aware of the impending arrival of Lady Mahj, but she had arrived a week early and no one had been prepared for that. Miles knew things would be very different with a lady in the manor, but he did not realize just how different it would be. As Isabel was thinking about her father's question, a loud bang caused by the kitchen door slamming against the wall startled her. The young count stalked into the kitchen, looking around the room, overturning the empty baskets, and looking through the bread as if someone had hidden something among the loafs.

"Can I help you find somethin', me lord?" Miles asked politely. "Goose! Do we have goose for supper?" he demanded. "Chicken, sir," Miles replied while opening the pot where it was simmering.

The count stared at the cook as if he did not understand.

"It's a different kind of fowl, sir," Miles added.

The young count grabbed his head with his hands and began rambling on, "No goose! This will not do. The lady Mahj is a woman of great refinement and has arrived a week early. We must have goose for supper. Goose is the fowl of nobles. We cannot serve her chicken. It is not a proper meal for such a lady."

Miles looked up at the panicking noble flailing his arms about the room and laid his hand on his shoulder and said softly, "Sir, I have known many nobles who have enjoyed such a fowl thing. The lady will like the chicken the way I will serve it."

A sadness fell upon the count as he sat on a free stool next to Isabel and cracked a half smile in her direction. "I know you mean well, Miles, but I mistakenly told her that we would have goose in her honor, without realizing that we had no goose. Now she will think me a buffoon when you serve her chicken instead. She may think us so coequal that I wouldn't know the difference from a goose and a chicken."

"I am sure she won't think that, me lord," Miles said knowingly as he walked over to the hearth, where an iron pot was stewing, and poured the contents into a cup and placed it in front of the count. "This will calm you down, me lord. 'Tis mint from the garden. I think I did see a goose drying at the Pickman house this morn. I can take a walk down and trade something for it, and we will have goose, me lord."

"I owe you a debt," the count said as he sipped the hot tea from the battered cup.

"No, sir, 'tis my pleasure to serve ya, sir," Miles said as he grabbed his coat and gave Isabel instructions.

Miles cared for the count and invited the chance to impress the new mistress. With his coat on, he walked into the garden and out the gate leading to the road that ran past the Pickman house. He knew the count could have demanded the goose but chose to give the people living in the town more freedoms. Miles knew that if he explained that the count needed the goose, Mr. Pickman would just give it to him, and that would be the end of it. In the end, Miles invited the Pickmans to enjoy a fine chicken dinner with fresh cherry pies for dessert at the manor house in exchange for the goose that would please the count.

Upon returning to the manor with the goose, Miles arrived to find Isabel talking to someone he did not know collecting the herbs in his garden. He leaned over the fence with the large bird on his shoulder.

"Who is this, Isabel?" Miles asked.

"This is Lady Mahj's servant. The lady wanted something to settle her tummy. We were just talking while the mint was stewin'," Isabel said.

"Don't keep 'em waitin' too long. I am sure he's gots things ta do," Miles said while bringing the goose into the house to cook.

After Miles placed the goose on the table, he watched and listened to the conversation between his daughter, Isabel, and the young boy who served the lady who would soon become the new mistress of the manor. As they spoke of the lady Mahj, a smile stretched across his face. He decided to make a special dessert that would please the lady, and in turn, he knew it would also please the duchess.

CHAPTER 3

YIELDING IN DARKNESS

The sun had gone down, and the manor was abuzz with activity. Mahj, the new mistress of the house, had arrived early, and the count, Elli, was trying to make everything perfect for her. Fayette was left in Mahj's room to finish sorting out her things while she was in the main hall for dinner. Mahj had always dreamed about marrying a great man who would win her heart through actions of love, but this man had done none of that. He had been chosen to marry her by the duchess in order to restore Mahj to her rightful place among the nobility through the association of the house of Bennu. Fayette toiled with her thoughts, knowing that marriage was forever and that a poor match would wreck Mahj's chances of finding someone who actually loved her.

Once the dinner had begun, the remaining guards were called to the hall to make a show for the new countess. Fayette was left alone for the first time since she had arrived. After folding the last of Mahj's dresses, she closed the door and peeked into the hallway. She looked up and down the hallway, but there were no guards to be found in either direction. This was her chance to see what kind of man this count was and what he had been up to. She quietly walked past the main stair to the far side of the manor to where the count's private chambers would be found.

An elaborate archway opened the way to the far end of the manor. The hall was lit by a regiment of candle fixtures along the walls to light the way to a large bay window overlooking the gardens. The window was framed with iron that had been curled and shaped to resemble roses. Red velvet lined the walls, with a multitude of color running along the entire length. It seemed elegant for a man who chose to outfit a room entirely in pink. The doors along the hallway were older and made of a heavier wood than the part of the manor chosen for Mahj. The moonlight shone above her head through panes of glass along the ceiling, giving the hall an outdoor feel.

Fayette knew she did not have much time before someone found her. She had to determine which of the doors was the one belonging to the count. A woolen runner covered the length of the hallway, which was pleasing to the eyes, but it was not new. Having lived in the house of the duchess, she knew there were always people coming and going to see the duchess in her private office adjacent to her chambers. She hoped the count had similar habits, and she began to inspect the rug for wear. Seeing nothing out of the ordinary, she slipped off her shoes and began to feel the rug with her feet. It was soft along the edges and coarse in the middle. Fayette closed her eyes and began to walk down the hall.

Seeing with the sensation in her feet alone, she came upon a large double door in the middle of the hall. *This has to be it,* she thought to herself. Standing on either side of the doors was a suit of armor holding a weapon that was exaggerated to a point that no real soldier would want to carry such a disproportionate weapon into combat. Upon closer examination, Fayette could see that the armor was not really designed to protect a man. Much like many other things in the manor, it was but a shell of a soldier from some nightmare realm and not from the real world at all. As she passed the tin golem, she placed her hand on the handle of the door and turned it.

As the door swung open, it let out a loud creak. In a moment of panic, she looked down the hall and listened. No one had been alerted to the awful sound. She went into the room and, as quietly as she could, closed the door behind her. There was a chair in front of a large window with a small bed that was not made. A small desk sat against one wall. A small wardrobe stood on the opposite wall. This, the room that was supposed to be an office, looked like it was being used as a separate bedroom adjacent to the count's bedroom. But whom was this room for? Who was the count hiding?

Fayette walked across the room and opened the wardrobe. *Perhaps,* she thought, *he has another woman that he is keeping secret.* She would have to tell Mahj, of course. As her hand rested on the handle of the door to the wardrobe, Fayette had a moment of delight at the thought of Mahj returning with her to the duchess's castle. She flung open the door and found men's clothing within. Fayette thought this very strange and began to look closer. They were not just a man's clothing but the clothing of the count himself. It was curious to see that he would use a small office as his bedroom when he had a large room available to him just beyond the great doors on the other side of the room.

Fayette sat on the bed for a moment, observing a cup sitting on the side table with a remnant of milk at the bottom. *If this is the bedroom of the count,* she wondered, *then what is behind those doors?* She got up from her resting place and walked across the room to the doors that would squelch her curiosity. She placed her hand on the handle of the door and turned it, but the door was locked. Looking frantically at the door, she noticed no lock and tried the door again. This time, with a sound that resembled a kiss, the door swung open effortlessly.

"Aha! What do we have here?" she exclaimed.

"That is the old nursery. Would you like to tell me what you are doing here?" When Fayette spoke, she had not expected to get an answer. She slowly turned around to see the disappointed face of Doris standing in front of her. "Answer quickly before I call a guard."

As she closed the door behind her, the color drained from Fayette's face, leaving it white with fear as she attempted to think of a good lie. She had been caught, but what could she say that would get her out of this jam?

Doris stood patiently awaiting an answer while tapping her foot, with her arms folded across her chest. She did not seem upset. She actually seemed amused by the whole affair.

"Why, you're not even a boy, are you?" Doris said while removing the hat that concealed Fayette's long hair.

With no other recourse, Fayette surrendered. "Mahj want—er, Lady Mahj wanted me to come with her. I am Fayette. The duchess thought that I should be sent dressed as a boy so that the eye of the count be not attracted to me. This union is very important, and we didn't want anything to jeopardize that."

Doris listened with skeptical resilience and said thoughtfully, "I see. And the duchess was right to do so, but why, then, are you in the young master's room? Surely you were not sent here to spy on my lord, for we have nothing to hide from her ladyship."

"Uh, no, of course, she wouldn't," Fayette lied like a greased slide. "It is true that the duchess is concerned with the kind of friends the count keeps, but in reality, I came in here to see what my dear friend Mahj was getting herself into with this man. I really don't know what she sees in him, I really don't."

"Well, that is the first true thing I have heard from you since we have met," Doris said. "Come now, I will make you some tea, and we can talk more about Lady Mahj."

Doris took the young woman's hand and guided her to the kitchen, where Fayette was given a special tea made for her to relax. Doris had hoped to loosen Fayette's tongue about the intentions of the duchess. Fayette was relieved that she was not in as much trouble as she expected to be in without having to reveal the duchess's plot. As she relaxed with Doris, she talked about Mahj and her deepened friendship with her, which put Doris at ease.

Meanwhile, across the shire, Dar was having difficulties of his own. With only a dim glimmer of light from the sky peeking through the treetops to guide him, Dar struggled to see where the path—any path—could be located beyond the thorny barrier of the bramble. While holding a torch in one hand to light the forest before him, Dar had been hacking his way through the thorns of the bramble wood with his sword for hours. Using what light he had, he searched for an animal path, but the forest was drinking every drop of light his torch gave, with nothing to remit. Dar was determined to break through the barrier that had protected the shores of Hibernia from invasion for centuries, but he grew tired.

His arms sore from the climb and now the heavy work of clearing a way through the wall of elder trees and thorny bramble that grew around them, Dar stopped to catch his breath. Wondering how far he still had to go before reaching a clearing beyond the rows of thorny vines, he stood on his toes and stretched as high as he could, lifting the torch above his head to see over the thick bramble; but he could only see the empty darkness ahead of him. He sat on the dirt and pulled his book from his pocket to review his map once more. Fearing that he might be lost, Dar set the book down and closed his eyes.

Although he could not see what had made the unearthly howl that disturbed his slumber, the presence of the large creature alerted his senses. He narrowed his eyes to see into the darkness but saw nothing. Quickly he extinguished the flame of his torch and waited for his eyes to adjust to the darkness. He sensed the creature right in front of him, but nothing came forward. He grew impatient and stood up and called to it, ready for anything.

"Come out and face me," he challenged it, but again, there was nothing.

As he stood in the pitch-black darkness, Dar's fears began to fill the void of his vision with images of creatures manufactured by his imagination. He stomped his foot, yet nothing stirred in the forest. Dar knew that whatever was there was waiting for the right moment to strike. Narrowing his eyes, he could almost see a pair of eyes looking at him. He lunged his sword into the brush that lay before him. His footing slipped on a mud patch, and he fell head over heels into the vines. He tossed and turned, struggling to get up, but soon his arms and legs started to get tangled in the vines of the bramble. The thorns of the vines began to pierce his skin.

"It's the bramble that's alive!" he shouted as it began to pull him in.

With the torch out and Dar's arms and ankles wrapped with the vines of the bramble, the brush seemed to enclose around him. As Dar turned around to see the way he had come, the brush closed around him. He was trapped within the brush. The more he struggled, the more it seemed to entangle him. Dar fought to escape the clutches of the strange foliage, but the vines tightened around his arms. As vines began wrapping around his chest, it soon pinned and drew him into the nexus of the plant.

Soon Dar was covered by some kind of green slime designed to devour him. Still unable to break free, Dar began to think about the small rabbit that had appeared by his side years ago. Seeing only the narrow leaves and vines of the dreadful plant, he wished that the rabbit were here to eat his way free; but alas, that rabbit was in Cornwall, and he was far away in Hibernia, lost in the wilderness. Closing his eyes, Dar imagined what horrors awaited him as his fingers and legs began to tingle, as if being air-dried after a good scrubbing with a straw brush. This was the first step of his transformation into foodstuff for plants. After a time, Dar allowed himself to drift away to avoid the expected digestion that awaited.

Still unable to move, Dar felt his body shifting, as if he were moving. The plant was creeping him away from the nexus for an unknown reason. Was this part of the process of his transformation? He wondered. Vines slapped his face and his bare legs where his trousers had torn as he effortlessly glided past them. A sense of panic fell over him as he imagined the many images of what horrors could be awaiting him. Dar struggled one way and then the next until he finally broke his arm free. Reaching over, he began to wipe the green sludge from his face to see. The plant was moving him, but to where was a mystery. Dar saw the snapping mouth of the weird plant, which seemed to be moving away from him.

With one arm free, Dar did not want to wait to see what new horrors awaited him. He reached down to his belt and removed a knife that had been tucked away for any unforeseen emergencies. Bringing the knife to his other arm, which was still wrapped in vines, he began cutting the tentacles of the hideous plant away. As Dar's body was somehow being pulled away, several tendrils shot from its nodes and clasped Dar's ankles to pull him closer once more. Breaking his left hand free, he began to cut the new tendrils from his ankles. As he cut the remaining vines, he was forcibly vomited from the hedge, and he landed on his hands and knees in front of the strange plant.

He slowly opened his eyes and found himself face-to-face with a large rabbit, who was sitting before him, happily chewing leaves that had gotten trapped in the folds of his clothing. Dar smiled as he experienced a moment of déjà vu from many years before.

"What are you doing here?" he asked, almost laughing at the irony.

Dar hadn't really expected the rabbit to answer; after all, it was just a rabbit. But as Dar began to stand, the rabbit put down the leaf he was eating. "What do you mean? You called for me."

"Where did you come from? Wait, how could you be talking to me?" Dar demanded suspiciously.

"Come on, I have always been with you. But I wasn't going to go in there after you, so I brought you here. But if you don't need me, then I will just...," the rabbit spoke matter-of-factly while waving a leaf around and began to fade from existence.

"No, wait! Don't go!" Dar shouted.

"Relax, I am here," he said while solidifying.

"What are you? I mean, rabbits don't talk, and you are clearly talking to me," Dar inquired.

The rabbit drew a deep breath. "How do you know that? Have you ever listened when an animal spoke to you? Nonetheless, I am part of you. A spirit, if you will. I was sent by your mother."

"My mother? She died when I was born."

"Yes, and she asked me to watch over you and here I am, at your service," the rabbit said as he bowed in a gentlemanly fashion. "Now wipe that green sludge from your face."

Dar screwed his face up while he brushed the slimy green film from his body and then turned to the rabbit, who was patiently waiting. "I seem to have gotten a bit lost. I am looking for a road that was supposed to be around here somewhere. Do you have knowledge of this place?"

The rabbit lifted his arm. "Do you mean that road there?"

Dar turned around to find a road cutting through the forest. It was not a regularly used road, for it was overgrown with weeds; but it was the road he was looking for. Dar grabbed the rabbit's paw and began shaking it wildly, thanking him for helping him. After being shaken off his feet, the rabbit fell to the ground and watched as Dar LaCross began running through the woods without his sword. Shaking his head, the rabbit, like gossamer, faded from existence once more with the forgotten sword.

Dar was relieved that he was finally headed to the city where the knights of Hibernia had made their home. He wanted to get there as fast as his legs could carry him, but he did not really have a sense of how far away the city was located. As he made his way through the unfamiliar forest, he imagined what he would say to the commander when they would first meet. He was certain he wanted to make a good first impression. He imagined he would tell him of his quest from Cornwall, and his pedigree was important, of course. Then he would dazzle them with his skill with his sword. That was when he realized his sword was not in its sheath.

Dismayed that he had lost his sword, he began to slow his stride to a stop. He folded over to catch his breath and looked into the forest behind him. There was a vast darkness behind him. Realizing that he would not be going back for it, he decided to push on. He felt foolish that he would forget such a thing of importance, but he did forget it. Knowing that he would have to replace it, he quickly checked his purse. After opening it and giving it a hasty glance, he was confident he would be able to buy a new sword once he reached the city. The city was still nowhere to be seen, but he knew that if there was a road, then the road must lead to the city. Off he went, continuing to follow the road.

As he walked the tattered road, Dar began hearing the birds singing in the trees. *Dawn must be close,* he thought. Then he would be able to review the book and see where he was going. Glad that he might be close, he began to run again.

Clanking along, Dar alerted the attention of two sentries who were charged with scouting the outskirts of the city. They spotted Dar running toward them on the path to the town. Once they had gotten themselves into position, they charged Dar. Running toward his flank on both sides, they tackled him and wrestled him to the ground.

"Who are you, and where do you think you be going?" one of the scouts demanded.

"I am Dar LaCross, and I am looking for the city," he answered.

Mistaking him for a farmer, they demanded to see his travel writ, which he did not have because he was not a farmer and not from Hibernia. Looking into the man's eyes, Dar simply said, "Take me to your leader."

"Oh, I am sure the count will have something to say about this," the scout replied.

Helping him up from the ground, the lesser scout took the bag from Dar's shoulder and carried it, in case it had something dangerous hidden within. The older of the two put his sword back into its sheath and ordered Dar to start walking. Exhausted from the events of the evening, Dar hesitated.

"How far is the city from here?" Dar asked.

The older scout removed a rope from his belt. "Now you're not going to give us any trouble, are you?"

"No, sir, that won't be necessary. I want to meet this count of yours," Dar replied.

The scout put the rope back into his belt and nudged Dar to motivate him to start walking. Dar began to walk in the direction the two scouts wanted him to go. The scouts each carried a sword and a bow over their shoulder. Dar was glad they did not decide to take a shot at him, because he did not anticipate an encounter with guards on his route to the city. He was glad he did not have his sword with him now that he was a prisoner of the count.

Prisoner or not, Dar was glad he would finally be brought to the city of the knights, where he would meet them and join them. He was sure they would accept him once they heard his story. The scouts were dressed very differently than Dar. They each wore dark-green cloaks to mask their appearance in the forest. Underneath, Dar observed fur bindings around the scouts' legs and forearms; hardened black leather bands were wrapped around their waists for protection against swords, and each wore a skirt he had previously read was the uniform of the day. As they led Dar toward the walled town, they thought he must be a crazy person, for he was smiling the entire way.

Soon they reached the edge of the forest, where dawn's light was peeking through the leaf-covered path. The smell of smoke filled the air. Taking in the light and the smells, Dar became excited that they must be near the famed city. The scouts, however, had picked up the pace, for they feared the worst. They knew that something was not right. The scouts became more agitated by the moment as they yelled for Dar to walk faster. Having had his arms and legs recently wrapped tightly by the strange plant, Dar found it difficult to move any faster through the thick of the forest where his guides were leading him.

The older of the scouts moved the branches aside to reach the clearing, only to find that the town was ablaze. The rear gates had fallen aside as the palisade had begun to buckle under its own weight after the fire had burned out the supports. The scouts stood horrified and motionless at the spectacle.

CHAPTER 4

At Dawn's Early Light

Dar heard screams coming from beyond the wall of flames. But what could he do? He was a prisoner of the two soldiers who had captured him in the woods and brought him here. He stood with the two men and wondered, Where were the knights to help the city? In Dar's recollection of the book he carried with him, these men should have been part of the knighthood, but as they discussed leaving the city to its own demise, he quickly realized that the knights were nowhere to be found.

"Aren't you going to do something?" Dar yelled at the two statues stunned by the sight.

As Dar waited for a response, the scouts returned Dar's bag and began to turn to leave the area.

Motivated by the continued screams of the townspeople from within, Dar pulled a sword from one of the scouts' scabbard standing beside him and charged into the fallen palisade. Flames were consuming every inch of the logs that made up the former wall. Dar looked back at his captors, urging them to follow, and then charged up the palisade, using it like a ramp. Sweat began beading down his face as he approached the wall of fire. As a ball of flames arose from underneath the fallen wall, Dar hesitated for a moment as the embers singed the ends of his hair.

After gathering his composure, Dar disappeared into the wall of fire that engulfed the opening to the town wall, and that was the last time the two scouts saw him. They turned to each other, and with a gesture, the older scout made it clear he was not going to follow and stalked past the other, returning to the darkness of the forest. The younger scout turned to look back to where the crazy young man had charged and, for a moment, placing his hand on the hilt of his sword, considered charging in after him. As he leaned forward, the other scout grabbed his arm to pull him back to reality.

"I know what you're thinking," he said, and as the other man opened his mouth to speak, he interrupted. "No!" The two men disappeared reluctantly within the safety of the forest, leaving the townspeople to whatever fate awaited them.

Meanwhile, the town was a burning chaos. The invaders had carpeted the thatched roofs of the sleeping town with flaming arrows within its great walls, setting the dried straw of the unsuspecting houses ablaze. As the smoke of the flames began to clear, Dar witnessed fur-clad men, who seemed wider than they were tall, carrying food and some furniture from the houses and running in all directions. The heat from the stone houses and wood houses created a flowing river of molten iron through the center of the road, spreading the fire to whatever it touched. Unable to ascertain who was an invader and who was a town person, Dar stood motionless while he watched people running in all directions.

As he carefully walked through the ever-growing ruin, Dar slowly made his way to what he imagined was once the town center, now burning out of control. Dar had never tasted the heat of a battlefield; but in his mind, he thought that if he had known what a battlefield looked like, it would look very much like what he was witnessing. As the assorted men were running from place to place, no one seemed to notice or care that Dar was standing around. No one in the town paid Dar any attention as he aimlessly wandered through the destruction. Houses collapsed in all directions while Dar noticed the sheer beauty of the burning town.

Black smoke billowed above the streets that crossed between the buildings and led to the square, where Dar was standing. Suddenly, he heard the unmistaken sound of clashing swords. He turned wildly from side to side while he looked for where the sounds were coming from. As he moved closer to the edge of the square, he heard the sound of men struggling from within one of the barns that stood on the edge of the town square.

As he listened through the door, it suddenly burst open as one of the fur-clad men flew through the door, breaking it off its hinges and reducing it to splinters, and landed in a ditch filled with sewage and waste. Dar timidly looked into the smoky darkness of the inside of the barn. Looking deeply, he spotted a large man wearing an apron and holding a broomstick while stalking the warrior who was now lying on his back. The warrior quickly got to his feet, pulling a double-bladed ax from the mud where it had landed, and began waving it around with malicious intent. Armed with his broomstick, the large man smacked the warrior on the forehead and stunned him. As the warrior sat in the cold filth and mud, the ax lay motionless as the apron-wearing man walked on by.

As Dar watched with amazement, it became apparent he would be the next victim of the broomstick, as the burly apron man began to walk intently toward Dar. Looking from side to side, Dar took a defensive posture. The large man readied his stance in front of Dar and, with a single motion, charged at him. Dar leaned to one side and dodged the raging man. Not wanting to hurt the man, Dar weaved and dove to avoid the wrath of the broomstick that had reduced the warrior to a lumbering mess.

"Stop," Dar cried out, "I don't want to hurt you!" He quickly took a blow to the head, which laid him flat before the raging man.

"Then why have you attacked us?" the man asked, with his foot holding Dar's chest to the mud.

"I haven't attacked anyone," he replied, gasping for air. "I only just arrived a moment ago! Is this the way you greet visitors?"

"What do you mean you only just arrived?" the man asked, pressing the remaining air from the poor boy's lungs.

"I am earnest when I say that I am not with those warriors." The words were choked out as Dar struggled to speak. "I arrived when I saw the fire."

The large man had an embarrassed look on his face as he helped Dar to his feet. No amount of apologizing could take away how bad he felt for knocking Dar to the ground. With one hand, Dar was lifted out of the mud and put on his feet. He had never before seen such a strong man.

"I am looking for my daughter," the large man said.

"The city is burning! Where would she have gone?" Dar inquired, eager to help the man.

The man looked at the manor, which was all but consumed by flames, and then to the barns, where he had been searching. He grabbed Dar and said, "If you will look in the manor, I will continue to look in the storehouses. If you find her, come and get me. Her name is Isabel."

"Wait, what is your name?" Dar called out while the large man began to run toward the barns.

"I am Miles, the cook," he said with a gleam in his eye as he turned to enter the smoking storehouse.

"If you're the cook, I would hate to meet the sergeant at arms," Dar said to himself.

Shoving his sword into the empty scabbard on his hip, Dar ran toward the burning manor. The heat from the building was terrifying, and black smoke billowed in all directions from its windows. He took a cloth from his pocket and covered his mouth with it as he went into the cloud of black soot flowing from the great double doors that once adorned the front of the grand edifice. Once inside, he could not see very much, but he heard voices coming from the back of the house. Dar was unfamiliar with the layout of the house and held out his hands to see where he was going. Feeling his way down the hallway, Dar reached the doors that led to the kitchen. Not knowing if it was a door or a wall, he gingerly gave it a shove. The door swung open to the grand kitchen, which was not yet on fire.

Pushing his way into the kitchen, Dar found a young man wearing fine clothing unconscious and lying on the floor next to the hearth. It appeared that he was holding an iron skillet in one hand and his scabbard was missing its sword. Dar checked to see if the man was dead by pressing his ear to his chest. Although Dar could not hear his heart beating, the man began to wake up, coughing and gasping for breath. Dar picked up a cup from the floor and ran over to a large pot that had been hanging over where the fire had been and scooped out some of the contents. He sniffed it to determine what it was and brought it over to the man lying on the floor.

Dar lifted the battered man's head and offered him the contents of the cup. The man grabbed his arm to steady the cup and took a drink.

"I tried to stop him, but I could not. I have failed to do even the smallest thing," the man said, sobbing.

"What happened here?" Dar asked while helping the man to his feet. "I met a man named Miles who said he was the cook. Is that who you are talking about?"

"The barbarian—a soldier, not the cook—came in, and I tried to stop him."

"Look, I don't know who you are, but I am looking for Isabel, the cook's daughter," Dar announced.

"He took her and ran that way toward the gardens." The man pointed.

Dar helped him to his feet and carried him out of the burning building. He showed Dar where the barbarian had taken the girl, and he thanked him repeatedly. Dar found a small patch of grass along the edge of the garden, where he thought the man should be out of sight from anyone wanting to bring him harm.

"What is your name, young sir? So I might reward you for your deed," the man asked.

"I am Dar LaCross. There is no need to reward me, sir. I am glad to perform my duty to save you, sir," he replied proudly, puffing out his chest.

"Well, Dar LaCross, I am Count Bennu." He paused as he looked around at the ruin of his domicile. "Elli Bennu." He stuck out his hand. "I will report well to the duchess about ya," the count said with a smile.

"Well, Elli, I will try to return to make sure you are safe, but I would get out of here as soon as you can walk." Dar shook the man's hand and then darted through the burning buildings where the count had indicated the warrior had taken Isabel.

Dar ran down a series of alleyways formed by the catch-as-catch-can building style of city planning, if there had been a city planner involved at all. He became nervous about the heated wooden walls falling in on him as he observed the buckling of the timber that towered over him. He gathered his fear and ran through the black smoke, which was filling every inch of the openings between the randomly placed buildings. For a moment, he worried he would not catch up with the barbarian in time to save the young girl. He covered his mouth again with his cloth and ran through the burning buildings.

Once he reached the open street on the other side of the burning mess, his eyes tearing and black streaks running down his face from the soot, Dar spotted a warrior carrying a screaming child over his shoulder. As fast as his legs could carry him, Dar flanked the warrior to knock him to the ground. The warrior, like Dar, could not see well from the clouds of smoke that were settling everywhere. He was disoriented and confused as to the direction he had to go. As he stood in the middle of a road wide enough for two wagons to pass, Dar ran as fast as he could into the unsuspecting barbarian. As he hit the man, Dar grabbed him around the waist, hoping the momentum would knock him to the ground and he would let go of Isabel. However, when Dar hit the man, it was like running into a large stone; he did not move. As Dar held on to him, the momentum flew Dar around him, causing the barbarian to lose his balance and fall over.

Lying in the mud opposite him, the warrior, who was sitting in a pile of sewage looking very cross with Dar, waited to see what his next move would be. He casually looked around for the location of his ax, as not to let Dar know he was without it. The girl, Isabel, was, for the first time since her abduction, quiet, from fear of what would happen next. With the girl standing between the two warriors, Dar looked around for something that would give him an advantage over the mighty barbarian. As the morning sun began to peek over the hills, a reflective glintcaught his eye. He struggled to make out what was shining in the sunlight. Then it dawned on him—it was the barbarian's ax.

Leaping up from the ground, Dar drew his sword and charged at the man sitting on the mud. Unarmed and fearing for his life, the barbarian searched for something to protect himself with. As Dar ran toward him, the warrior rolled toward a pile of hay that had been stacked for the town the day prior. He grabbed a pitchfork from its resting place and spun around to face his adversary. As he positioned himself in a sure-footed stance with his fork in hand, he watched as Dar grabbed the girl and ran down the smoke-filled street. Looking around at the total lack of assailants, he casually strolled over to retrieve his ax and ran toward the breach where the burning wall had collapsed, making way for an easy escape.

Standing at the wagon that had brought them to Teamhrach, Fayette worked to make certain that Mahj was safe. When Fayette had noticed the attack from Mahj's second-floor bedroom window, she had run down to alert their host. The count had called for his guard and left Mahj to meet the invaders. Knowing that the town was already on fire, Fayette took Mahj by the hand and raced to the barracks, where their guards had been sent. From the dining room, it was an easy run to the main door, where they were met by the old sergeant who had greeted them when they first arrived.

"We have to get ya out of here!" he yelled as he placed a wet blanket over her to protect her from the flames of the manor.

They ran to where the wagon had been stored, and as they crossed the courtyard, the younger of their guards had run past them toward the house. Fayette called to him, and he joined the three in the barn.

The two guards had been making the wagon ready for a hasty escape when Miles had wandered in to ask if Isabel was with them. She was not. Fayette feared the worst for poor Isabel. She placed Mahj inside the wagon as the guards were ready to leave.

"Miles, I will find her! I know where she may have gone. Will you please look after Mahj for me and keep her safe?" Fayette pleaded.

"No, Fayette! You have to stay with me," Mahj wailed.

"Yes, but please find Isabel! When the wagon is clear from the town, I will return to meet you. Look for us at the reservoir along the south road. Do you know the place?" Miles said.

"I know the place. Don't worry, I will find her," she replied.

"No, Fayette! You will be killed," Mahj interrupted.

"Look, Mahj, you need to get back to the duchess. I don't know what is happening here, but she will need to know. I have to find that little girl! Now go!" Fayette ordered.

The younger guard looked very confused as he watched Fayette run out of the barn and into the road. He had his orders to keep Fayette safe. He thought at the time that it was curious the duchess would give such an order for Fayette and not for Mahj, but here she was, running off into certain danger. What would he say to her? What would she say to him? As the young guard stood up to climb off the wagon, the old sergeant grabbed him to shove him back into his seat atop the wagon as they rolled out into the square, heading for the main gates.

Seeing that the manor was ablaze, Fayette ran around to the rear, where the kitchen entrance was. When she rounded the manor, she saw the count walking away, using a broken fence post as a cane to walk. As she ran toward him, he became startled and turned around wielding the post like a sword to defend his person. He was relieved to see it was his bride's serving boy.

"Ah, good, it's you. Has Mahj gotten away safely?" he asked, noticing that her hair was hanging down, revealing that she was not a boy after all.

"Yes, she is fine! The guards took her away to bring her back to Eamhain. You best get out of here too. Did you see Isabel?" Fayette inquired.

"Yes, a barbarian attacked me and carried her off. They headed in that direction. Can you help me get out of here?" But as he finished his sentence, she was already running toward where she had spotted the breach in the wall where the invaders had come from.

Fayette wanted to avoid the clusters of burning buildings, so she ran over to the wall, where a ladder was constructed for soldiers to reach the catwalk along the top of the wall. She was agitated that the "highly trained soldiers" the count had boasted about upon their arrival were nowhere to be found. She searched the streets below, hoping to see a man carrying the small girl, but she found nothing. (By this time, the invader had fled the burning town.) She turned and then searched the tree line for Isabel.

Below the wall, she spotted a man carrying a small screaming girl. *This has to be her,* she thought. *The man is carrying a sword, so he is a soldier.* The encumbered soldier was running along the base of the wall, searching for something, but she did not want to wait to find out what it was. Fayette ran along the catwalk to catch up to the encumbered soldier. As she found a spot where she could climb up on the wall's edge, she scaled the wall without the thought of her safety in mind. Running atop the wall's edge, she began catching up to the soldier below. Fayette took a deep breath and leaped off the wall.

As she dropped to the ground below, Fayette's mind began to work at lightning speed, giving her the perception that she was falling in slow motion. It was in these moments that her mind began to realize the gravity of what she had just done. Freeing her mind of fear, she opened her cloak in an attempt to guide her descent. She wasn't sure it was working, but it made her feel better anyway.

Fayette landed on the soldier who was carrying the girl. As Isabel went head over heels into the grassy knoll outside the walls of the town, she screamed at Fayette to stop. Fayette, who was bound and determined to rescue her from the clutches of the barbarians who had set the town ablaze, found herself lying in a pile of sewage that had piled against the wall of the great town. The rather small barbarian was facedown in the dirt, mumbling unintelligibly at her. When she jumped from the high ledge, her brain had been in high gear, which led her to jump; but now that she was on the ground again, she realized she did not have a plan. She ran over to the little girl, who was pointing at the man who was getting up from being facedown in the mud.

Dar, who felt very indignant, worked to get himself up from the ground after having a woman drop on him from above. He had not expected such a surprise when he had snatched the little girl from her captor. He walked over to the little girl to see if she was hurt while holding his arm out, which was theuniversal symbol for "I had enough." As he knelt down and the words were formulating in his mouth, the flying lady jumped on his back, screaming. He jumped up and staggered around with Fayette on his back, yelling for her to get off.

"You stay away from her!" Fayette yelled, riding Dar like a bull while hitting him on the head with her fists.

"Ouch, hey! What are you doing? I am one of the good guys! I am here to help!" he yelped and then fell down again.

Fayette landed on her butt on the dirt. "Here to help? What?" "Yes, most people introduce themselves before jumping on them.

I guess you are an extraordinary being," he said sarcastically. "I have to get you both out of here before we are spotted."

Dar picked up the little girl from where she was standing, set her on his hip, and ran into the forest. Fayette, having been left, followed Dar into the forest without an argument. Fayette had never been in the forest around the town before; she had not been in the town long enough to even know how to get to the south road from where they were. Although Fayette had never seen him before, the man carrying Isabel seemed to know where he was going. That was fine with her for the moment, but she knew she had to meet Miles and the carriage on the south road. Just as she gathered the courage to stop the man and ask, he stopped walking abruptly and turned around to face her.

"I have to go back into the city to tell Miles that I found her," Dar said.

"No, I..." She gathered her thoughts.

"You should be safe enough out here with Isabel. I have to go back and bring your husband out here so we can all leave together," Dar explained.

"Excuse me, sir, but—"

"Dar," Dar interrupted.

"Dar what?" Fayette asked.

"My name is Dar," he replied.

"What makes you think that Miles is my husband, Dar?" Fayette asked flippantly.

"You seem to have strong ties with the girl here, so you must be her mother," Dar explained. "Or are you just a crazy person jumping off the top of the wall like that?"

"I am not her mother. Did you just call me crazy?" The world was about to end for Dar if he did not think fast.

"If you are not her mother, then—"

"Don't even go there." As Dar watched her face turn red, he could almost see steam flowing from her ears. "I told Miles that I would meet him on the southern road outside the town. There is a carriage and soldiers there waiting," Fayette explained. "Do you know how to get to the King's Road?"

Dar looked up at the morning sky and saw which direction the sun had risen and said, "Yes, I think I can manage that." He assumed the south road was south of Teamhrach.

The King's Road (or the south road, as it is known to farmers and traders) meandered through the middle of the Marche connecting most of the farming communities, creating a divide through the foothills and ending in the broken lands. Because it went through the hills, it was not well-known and was only used by the farmers and herders. The nobility avoided it, and invaders had no knowledge of it at all. The nobility used direct routes, and invaders saw Hibernia as a land of no roads at all. Fayette had often traveled the road with the duchess, as she would visit the farmers to bless their fields. She was concerned that the soldiers would have less familiarity and would not be at the agreed-upon location when she arrived there, and by her recollection, this odd man was guiding them in the wrong direction.

"Excuse me," Fayette interjected.

"Dar," he replied.

"Oh dear, I think we are heading in the wrong direction," she pointed out.

"What makes you think that?" Dar asked while consulting with his book as the little girl rested on a moss-covered stone.

"If the town was that way,"—Fayette pointed through the vast forest—"then we should be traveling in that direction to get to the road."

Dar closed his book and consented to her tone of certainty. The truth was that Dar had only guessed what direction they should be traveling. After several hours of walking through the forest, he had hoped they would come across a road by now. Having come from Cornwall, Dar never imagined a forest so large could ever really exist. As Dar looked around, the forest looked the same in all directions. He even noted that some of the rocks they had passed looked much like other rocks they had already passed. He silently feared they had been walking in circles.

After resting for a time, Dar lifted Isabel onto his back, and they were off, blazing a trail through the forest once again. Fayette was grateful for Dar traveling with them. Isabel was tired and mostly slept while being carried by the tireless young soldier who had found them. Fayette did not mind carrying the bag of the young man, but she began to wonder where he had come from. As she followed him, she saw that his clothing was not of that she was accustomed to seeing. As they walked, she peeked inside his bag and found it filled with what looked like cooking equipment. She began to wonder why someone would carry an entire kitchen with them. In addition to that, he seemed intent on getting Isabel to her father, but she was sure he was not from the town.

After they had walked for many hours, they came across a small hut in the woods. When Dar spotted it, he stopped and turned to Fayette. He wondered if the hut belonged to those who attacked the town. Without a word, Fayette rolled her eyes at Dar and walked past him toward the mysterious hut, leaving him to stand there watching her move fearlessly toward what might be waiting within. Fayette placed the bag down next to a large fire ring with an iron cauldron hanging at the center of three iron hooks and walked up to two rotted boards that had been nailed together to pass as a door to some but that still had openings, leaving very little for someone looking for privacy. Dar put the young girl down and watched as Fayette knocked on the door. After a few moments of waiting, an old woman opened the door and greeted the weary travelers.

"Hello, I am Fayette, and this is Dar. We are on our way to the duchess. May we have lodging for the night?" she asked with a jovial air about her.

"I don't have much to offer to eat, but yer welcome to share what's I got," she said.

Fayette thanked the old woman in the old way by grabbing her at the elbows and leaning in toward her. Dar had never before seen this and watched with interest. When it was his turn, he became awkward, and the old woman simply welcomed him into her home. Once inside, the old woman began to create a small bed for Isabel to sleep in. Fayette started looking through her herbs. Having worked in the kitchen of the duchess, she had a small knowledge of what properties most herbs had. While Dar was busy getting Isabel settled in, Fayette selected a rather rare herb and hid it in her pocket. Meanwhile, she began to stir what was in a large pot simmering on the fire.

"I was just about to have supper. I am glad to have visitors. Are ya hungry?" the old woman asked.

Isabel perked up. "Yes, please."

The old woman collected three wooden bowls from an improvised cupboard and began to pour soup into each one with a large spoon. As she filled them, she handed each one to Fayette, who was at the ready to receive the bowls of nourishing goodness. Upon receiving the first bowl, Fayette inspected the contents and smelled it for hidden spices. Satisfied that it was merely a collection of boiled roots, herbs, and vegetables that were common to the area, she handed it to Isabel, who was already reaching for it. With the next bowl, Fayette slipped some of the herb she had picked up off the counter and stirred it in before handing it to Dar. After receiving the last bowl, Fayette sat down across from Dar and began to enjoy her meal with her companions. Fayette did not know Dar and still had many questions about where he was from and why he was in the Marche. She suspected that he either came with the invaders or was followed by them. Soon she would learn all.

After eating some soup, Isabel was ready to nap. She curled up on a bed that would have been better described as a shelf and closed her eyes. Dar and Fayette sat next to the fire with the old woman and engaged in idle chitchat. Dar began enthusiastically describing the beauty of what he had seen since he arrived in Hibernia, never divulging where he had come from.

"I was on my way to the city to meet with the knights when I saw the fire," Dar began.

"You came for the what?" the old woman inquired.

"You know, the old knights that were based there," Dar replied, unconsciously gesturing to his book.

"I think he means the specially trained soldiers of the count. He had been training farmers to prepare them for war to liberate the region when we were attacked," Fayette interjected. "So what is that thing that you kept looking at while we were walking?"

"Nothing. Just a book I brought from home," Dar evaded. Having worked with the chamberlain at the castle, Fayette was familiar with books, although they were not a common thing. The chamberlain had books containing old knowledge and, she imagined, some magic as well. She could only speculate what esoteric knowledge could be hidden away in the small book carried by this young buffoon. She began to imagine that Dar must be some kind of thief who had helped himself to a secret book from the library of some ancient kingdom. And she was half right.

As they were talking, Dar found he was falling asleep while talking. He imagined that he must have been more tired than he had thought. As he dozed off, he tried to remember when was the last time he had slept. He shook his body awake and asked for a cup of water. The old woman did not have any cups but went to get him a deerskin that was hanging on the wall containing water that she had collected from the nearby spring just that morning. By the time she had returned to Dar with it, he was fast asleep.

"Was that necessary?" the old woman asked of Fayette.

"Look, we were under attack all night and Teamhrach was burned to the ground and this guy just shows up. I don't know him or where he really came from. I came here for a wedding, and now I have to report to my lady that the whole area was attacked by who-knows," Fayette ranted while waving her arms about.

With Dar sound asleep, Fayette took the opportunity to search through his pockets and find out what this mysterious book was about. In his pocket, she found five pieces of black root, which she left, and the book. Taking the book, she sat down next to the fire and carefully opened it. She thought it might have some kind of magic and did not know what to expect. Holding it away from her face, she opened the cover to the page that had been dislodged from the rest. She expected something dramatic, but it was just a book after all. Putting it on her lap, she looked at the page. To her, not knowing how to read and having never opened a book before, it looked like a bunch of unintelligible, squiggly lines. Even the map that Dar used religiously was unidentifiable to her. Thinking this must be important, she decided to bring it to the duchess.

Shoving the book into her pocket just as Dar had done many times before, she took his bag and turned it upside down to empty the contents onto the dirt floor of the hut. The old woman watched with amazement as Fayette meticulously studied each item in Dar's bag. There was flint and steel for starting fires, a bedroll, rope, and a pair of trousers. She also found a small knife in the bag—not one that would be suitable for protection, but a knife merely for eating. She examined his trousers for a clue as to what might have made them. She noted that, like her, his clothing was made to look like a peasant's clothing but was cut from fine linens—a deception that only a concerned eye would have caught. At the bottom of the bag was a velvet money purse. Fayette opened it and found ten gold and three silver coins. Fayette had never seen someone reckless enough to carry such wealth on his person. She tossed it next to where Dar was sleeping peacefully.

The bulk of the bag had been occupied by two flat large iron discs. When she had first seen them resting in the bag, she assumed they were iron cooking pans, but as she was able to get a better look at them, she realized they were something different. They had been hammered flat, removing any lip that they might have had. The two discs were fastened together with heavy hemp ropes weaved through fur patches. She could not imagine why anyone would be dragging such heavy things through the forest. From what she could infer from Dar, he was not a man of forethought. The heavy discs had a kind of crest she did not recognize painted on one side in a paint that even now was chipping off.

With the book in her pocket for the duchess, Fayette awoke the little girl and prepared for them to leave. The old woman gave her a blanket, which she wrapped Isabel in as she unraveled the tightly wrapped locks of Fayette's hair with her small fingers. The old woman walked over to the table and began to turn some bread and cured meat in strips of cloth. Adjusting her clothing, Fayette took Isabel by the hand and headed for the door. As she turned back, the old woman handed her the wraps with a content but broken smile.

"And what of your friend? Will you just leave him here?" the old woman inquired.

"He is not my friend. I don't even know where he came from. He should wake up in a few hours, just tell him to go home," Fayette answered.

"Just head that way toward the smoke and then follow the road. That will take you to where you need to be," said the old woman, pointing to the black cloud on the horizon. With a glimmer in her eye, the old woman wished her well on her journey and returned to her sewing and waited for the young man to wake up.

Fayette did not know where she was exactly, but she was certain Dar had taken her in the wrong direction. Watching the sky, the two travelers followed a small animal path that was hardly visible to one who was not looking for it. Isabel, unaware of any danger, walked along humming a tune, which gave Fayette a lift in her feet as she walked along.

"We will get you to your father soon, little one," Fayette said while smiling.

Isabel curled Fayette's hand against her face and smiled a smile that would lead one to believe that she knew all would be well. As the old woman watched from the window, the two were gone from sight after a few moments.

After sleeping for a few hours, Dar sat upright and awoke with a gasp. His breathing was deep and heavy as he struggled to catch his breath. Having felt a gentle hand on his shoulder, he turned around wildly to be greeted by the old woman holding a tin cup of water. The cup was cold and felt damp to the touch as he accepted the cool, refreshing taste of water. After catching his breath, he noticed the contents of his bag were in a heap on the floor. He quickly looked from side to side.

"She's gone," the old woman said with just a hint of remorse. "What do you mean 'she is gone'?" Dar's brain was taking longer than normal to get running; his eyes were still spinning.

"The woman and the little girl left a little while ago," the old woman replied while walking over to something she had been brewing herbs for when he had woken up.

He stood up to walk over to collect his things but lost his balance as he swayed to one side. The old woman caught him and set him down in her rocking chair and returned to the hearth to fill a bowl. Dar felt sick. He buckled over and began coughing as if he would vomit a frog from the depths of his throat. The room was spinning as the old woman took his hands and pressed a wooden bowl into them. He looked at her despairingly.

"Drink it," she said.

Dar took his nose over the bowl and looked in it. It looked like wet mud with a rainbow slick running through the middle of it. The smell was vile and offended the nose and made him gag. The old woman gestured for him to drink it down. Dar held his breath and drank the concoction in one gulp. It tasted like dirt and rotting wood and caused him to gag as it slithered down his throat, looking for his stomach.

"Oh gods, woman! What was that? It tasted like dirt and slime!" Dar exclaimed.

"Dirt and slime," the old woman joked. "It will make you feel better. Just the hair of the dog. Now sit there till your eyes can adjust, and you will be fine."

Dar did not listen to her. He crawled over to his gear and began to inventory everything in the pile on the floor. The floor seemed to be moving in odd directions without him. He rolled over and saw the walls looking like they might melt at any moment.

"I can't believe she would rob me. After I helped her escape the city and brought her to safety, she robs me. I can't believe it," Dar exclaimed. Dar carefully placed everything into the bag.

"I came here to join the knighthood, and all I have found was one sieged and burning city and no sign of any knights. Do you know where I may find them? I am sure they will want to know of the attack," Dar asked.

"I know not of any knights that roam these lands," she said. "They protect this land. Men in armor. They are superior soldiers,"

Dar explained as if she were a child. As the old woman began to explain, Dar began seeing strange things. The ears of the old woman appeared to have grown points on them. Vines began to grow out from her clothing. As he listened to her speak, he shook his head to better concentrate on her words.

"The lord of this land is the great King Aviticus. I know it doesn't look like much, but he owns it all. He lives at the city on the Baile. It's by the sea. I am guessing that you will want to go there and tell him of the attack, and he will send his soldiers," the old woman explained.

"Ah, the city by the sea, this was the city that I was looking for," he said while reaching into his pockets. "I can report to him and then join his knights." A panicked look came over him, and he frantically began searching all his pockets. As he emptied the contents, he soon realized that the book was gone.

The old woman walked over to where Dar had been sleeping and found his velvet purse. Clearing her throat, she handed it to Dar, who quickly opened it and began to count his coins. His eyes softened after making sure his money was intact.

"Perhaps not a thief, me lord," the old woman said.

Dar began looking through the rest of his gear and reached into his bag one more time. Reaching around, he did not find the book and began to replace his gear in the bag. As he resumed packing, he looked up at the old woman.

"Yup, a thief. A thief of the worst kind. A book thief," he said. "There is a special hell for people who take books and don't give them back. How long ago did she leave? I must find her."

"You have plenty of time," she said with a suspicious grin. "She and the little girl are not going anywhere." She hesitated. "So not joining the knights then?"

Dar screwed up his face while he wondered just what she meant by that, and he began to stand up slowly. She handed Dar the tin cup once more and told him to drink it. He was relieved to find that it was only water. As he prepared himself to leave the hut, he put the bag on his back and began to center it in the small crevice of his spine. The old woman handed Dar the deerskin.

"Are you trying to drown me? I can't drink any more water. Thank you, but I have had enough," Dar said.

"Please take it. When you find her, she will need it," she said and handed it to him again. He took a second glance at her as she began to look younger to him. *It must be that concoction she made me drink,* he thought. He rubbed his eyes and took the deerskin, placing it over his shoulder. With a smile, he turned and walked out of the hut.

After taking a few steps, he stopped and thought of the kindness given to him by the stranger. He took a gold coin from his purse, felt the weight in his hand, and turned around to hand it to her, but he did not see the old woman. He walked back into the hut and looked around. The hearth was cold, the table was dusty, and the fresh herbs that had been drying were old and withered. It was as if the woman had never been there.

Dar slowly took the coin and placed it on the table and turned toward the door. A gust of wind passed him and blew the door open with a loud slam against the side of the hut. Dust fell from the ceiling. A voice drew his attention as he turned around.

"That is very kind of you, but what would I do with a gold coin?" the old woman asked, almost unable to be seen standing in front of a mud-covered wall. She walked over and took his hand and placed the coin back in his palm.

"D'oh, you're right," he said as he fumbled with his purse to retrieve a greater sum. "Maybe you can use this to get a nice place so you don't have to live in the forest?"

"Perhaps I am just an old witch who prefers to live in the woods?"

Dar's eyes leaped out of their socket as he noticed a slot on her forehead open and close to reveal a third eye. He rubbed his eyes again, and the face of the old woman returned to normal. *It must be the herbs again,* he thought to himself.

"You keep your coins. I won't be needing them, but I will remember your gentle kindness and how you have honored a poor old woman living alone in the woods," she said with a voice that almost sounded like an echo from a dream.

As he stepped toward the door, he heard the voice of the old woman in the wind, "Hurry, Dar LaCross, Fayette needs you." As suddenly as he heard it, she was once again gone. With great haste, Dar ran from the hut in the direction that Fayette and the little girl had gone, and he disappeared into the forest.

CHAPTER 5

THE WRONG ROAD HOME

Fayette and Isabel walked for hours, and there was still no sign of the road. The cloud of smoke they had been following had drifted with the air currents and had guided the intrepid travelers farther into the forest. Isabel was getting hungry and began to wonder why they had left without their guide. Fayette, continuing to walk, feared she was getting lost.

"Are we going back for the man who saved us?" Isabel asked.

"No, we are not. He is a stranger and may not be a good man," Fayette replied. She did not know what kind of man Dar was, but she was sure he had secrets. That made him dangerous.

"I can't go any farther! I'm too tired," Isabel said and sat down in the dirt.

Fayette did not know what to do. Isabel was too heavy for her to carry, and their location was too unfamiliar and exposed for them to rest where they were. She needed Isabel to travel just a little farther so they could at least reach the road, but she was not sure just where the road was.

"We are almost there. Your father is waiting for us," Fayette pleaded with the little girl. She took her hand to help her get up, but instead Isabel flopped on the ground, forcing Fayette to yank on her outstretched arm.

"No! I don't want to go!" Isabel yelled.

Fayette realized she had to try to negotiate with the child. "Isabel, your father is waiting for us. You want to see him, don't you? Can we just walk to that ridge?" Fayette pointed. "Just to that ridge, and then we can take a break and eat something. Will that be all right?"

"But my feet hurt," Isabel said as she stood up and grabbed Fayette's hand.

"I know, sweetheart. I know," she said to the little girl.

They had been walking for a very long time. Fayette knew the road had to be close, but she was still unable to see it. Fumbling through the forest, they came upon a large area of shrubbery. Fayette and Isabel got very close to the ground as they forced their way through the shrubs to reach the other side. As Fayette crawled on her hands and knees, they soon reached the other side. As she began to unfold herself, she noticed the road stretched before her. She was feeling very proud of herself as she helped Isabel out from beneath the bushes.

"Let this be a lesson to you, Isabel. Resourceful women do not need a man to do things for them. We are strong enough to do things on our own," Fayette schooled.

"He was nice, don't ya think?" the observant young girl asked.

"Yes, he seemed nice enough," Fayette answered without thinking.

"And he was cute too," Isabel said.

Fayette ignored the statement and continued to walk along the road, scanning for the wagon that was supposed to be waiting, but she saw no trace of the wagon or anyone else. She was certain they were close enough to at least run into survivors of the town who should be heading to the castle or at least to the next town, but there was no one.

After a few moments' rest, Isabel was ready to walk a little farther. Fayette scanned the horizon, looking for the soldiers, but the road was deserted. She wasn't sure how far she would have to walk, but she was glad she would not have to explain why to the little person happily humming at the end of her arm.

Isabel really did not mind the walk; there were pretty flowers to keep her occupied. Soon she dropped Fayette's hand and began to walk ahead of her on the road. Like a hawk, Fayette scanned the forest, hoping they would not run into the invaders that attacked the town.

As the elevation of the road increased and a sheer drop-off began to follow them on one side of the road, Fayette was pretty sure she had no idea where she was. The forest towered over them on both sides of the road, making it impossible to view the countryside, even with the drop-off. Isabel ran from flower to flower as roses bloomed on the inside of the road closest to the hill incline.

"Are we almost there yet?" Isabel checked in, holding a bouquet of roses in her hand.

"I am not sure, honey. I have never been on this road before." Satisfied with her answer, Isabel ran ahead on the road, collecting more flowers from their path. She seemed happy enough that she was not concerned with where they were headed, but Fayette had a growing concern. She did not know where she was and did not know where the invaders had come from. She was worried they might be walking right into where the enemy was. Still dressed like a peasant boy, she was certain that if they wandered into an enemy encampment, they would not give her and Isabel a second look. She hoped.

Soon the road was narrowing, and the forest thinned out, if not for the random tree growing out from the hillside. Isabel was skipping almost too far ahead of Fayette. Fayette called for her to walk closer to her, but Isabel continued ignoring her pleas. Fayette was getting tired and still did not recognize where she was walking. Deep crevices formed small fissures across the road, which they walked over. Fayette began looking at her feet instead of watching where she was walking.

Suddenly, she walked across a thin strand of spiderweb that Isabel was too small to have disturbed. Unaware of what the thing was that wrapped itself around her face, Fayette began screaming and turning in circles while waving her hands in the air to fend off whatever the thing was that she could not see. Losing all composure, she spun around and lost her balance. Still waving her arms about, she suddenly stepped off the side of the road into one of the fissures along the drop-off. Isabel ran to her screaming, but Fayette was lodged deep in the crevice.

Isabel was in a panic as she attempted to crawl down into the fissure to reach Fayette, but Fayette yelled to her to stop.

"Don't come any closer!" she screamed. "You have to stay there and watch for someone who can help me out."

With her new and very important job, Isabel began looking up and down the road, giving a careful eye to anyone who might be traveling along just as they had been. Fayette took the bag off her shoulder and threw it up to Isabel and told her to eat something.

Fayette was quite cross with herself. First, she had gotten lost, and now she was quite stuck and unable to climb out. She worried that the road had been quite desolate and that they could be stuck there for quite some time.

After several hours, Fayette's legs had gotten numb, and she could no longer move her feet. She listened as Isabel sang songs, making up lyrics of her friend being stuck in a hole, and after the tenth time hearing it, she worried she would soon lose her mind. Suddenly, Isabel went silent. Fayette worried something would happen to her, for she would not be able to help.

"Hey, Isabel, are you all right?" Fayette called up, but there was no response.

"Isabel!" she yelled.

As she looked up to the sky with real fear that something had happened, a face appeared in the opening of the fissure. It was the sprite face of Isabel.

"Someone is coming," she said and then quickly disappeared from view.

"Get them to help me out of here," Fayette called to the empty air.

Fayette struggled to listen but heard nothing. She began to worry that someone could have just taken little Isabel away. She struggled to try to climb out of the fissure but could not.

Moments passed without hearing the voice of Isabel. Fear began weaving stories of woe through her head that something unforeseen had happened to Isabel. Fear-stricken, her calm began to unravel, and she was reduced to a mad woman clawing at the walls, trying to dislodge herself from her predicament. She began screaming for help, but none would come.

Not knowing what fate had befallen Isabel and being unable to climb out of the fissure, Fayette sank into a deep sadness. She heard no sounds of people coming to help her and could not hear the voice of Isabel. She was feeling very alone as tears began to form in her eyes. Thoughts of her demise began to consume her thoughts. Would anyone even know to look for her? she wondered.

What seemed like an hour had passed when suddenly the face of Isabel appeared in the crevice opening and a man's voice was heard.

"She's down here," Isabel said. "Help her, please. We have been stuck here all day. I am sure she is sorry."

The pleas of the little girl were confusing to Fayette. *Who could she be talking to?* she wondered. Soon the familiar smiling face of Dar LaCross appeared in the opening of the fissure.

"Got yourself stuck, did you?" Dar asked in a joking manner.

"Will you just get me out of here?" Fayette demanded.

"Not so fast. You have stolen something from me, and I want it back," Dar bargained. *It is the book, he wants the book,* Fayette thought.

"Get me out of here, and I will give it back to you," Fayette agreed.

"I don't know," Dar said.

"What!"

"How about this: You hand me my book, and I will think about pulling you out?"

You venomous, pock-blackened toad, Fayette thought to herself. "You promised to save her!" Isabel screamed and began crying. "Fine! You win. I will hand the book up, and you will get me out of here," Fayette agreed.

She struggled to reach into her pocket, which was being pressed by the rocks along the crevice wall. With two fingers, she managed to slip the book from her pocket and passed it up to the void. Dar's hand retrieved the book and disappeared from view. After a few moments of nothing, Fayette began to get impatient.

"You said you would get me out! Hello, are you up there?" she called into the nothingness. *They wouldn't just leave, would they?* she wondered. Becoming very cross, she tried to twist herself loose but could not.

"Did you leave me?" she screamed.

Soon Dar dropped a rope with a loop tied in it over the very stuck body of Fayette. "Loop this under your arms," Dar instructed.

"What's going on?" Fayette demanded.

"Do you want to be out or not?" Dar asked.

Fayette did as she was instructed, and soon the rope began to tighten around her. The strength of Dar began to pull her one direction and then the next, but she was stuck for sure. She tried to yell up to Dar that it was not working, but there was no acknowledgment from above. Soon the rope began to pull her toward the opening of the crevice and toward certain death. She started to panic and began yelling, but the pull was too strong. Soon she was free and craning over the cliff. Dar leaned on the opposing end of the branch where he had tied the rope and forced Fayette back onto the ground, where Isabel was reaching for her.

Fayette was happy to be back above ground again but was angry with Dar just the same. She stood up and limped over to where he had been standing and smacked him as hard as she could. "Were you just going to leave me down there?" she yelled. "What is wrong with you?"

Dar started laughing. He had never planned on leaving her. As Dar approached, Isabel had run down to him and explained her predicament. He was very concerned and had asked for all the details, but before Isabel led him to where Fayette had fallen, he had to promise to her that he would save Fayette. Dar was more than happy to comply with the demands of the small overseer who then guided him to the fissure. Soon Isabel was making all sorts of demands of Dar as he began to devise a way to free the helpless Fayette from her prison.

Having been stuck in the sun for most of the day, the two women were dehydrated, and as the old woman from the hut had said, they needed the extra water he had been carrying. As the sun began to set on the horizon, they rested on the rocks that peppered the edges of the road. After eating the snack food that Dar had brought, Isabel curled into a ball and fell asleep. As the stars illuminated the sky, Dar took his book and walked to the edge of the cliff to determine where they were. Fayette, fully recovered from her ordeal, got curious about the thing and walked quietly up from behind Dar and craned over his shoulder.

"What is that anyway?" she inquired, referring to the book cradled in Dar's hands.

"It's a codex of some kind. Its importance is beyond my understanding, but I find it useful at times," he explained.

"A codex? I am not sure that I understand what that is."

"I am not sure that I could explain it. The shaman where I am from says that it contains my destiny, whatever that means. It contains stories of your home here and the knights of Hibernia that protect the people of this land," Dar explained.

"Where are you from? We don't have shamans here. The knowledge of my people lies with the druids. They hold the knowledge of the world itself," Fayette explained.

"I am from Cornwall. It's a land beyond the sea. I traveled here to join the knights. The old woman told me that I might find them in a place called the Baile on the coast, but now saving you has brought me farther inland than I wanted to be. I fear that I may never make it back to the coast."

"Yes, there are a lot of soldiers at the Baile. They might even be the soldiers who attacked and burned Teamhrach, the town where you found us. I don't know why you would want to join them anyway. Hey, I never had a chance to thank you for saving us. You could have left us out here," Fayette said while putting her arm around Dar's shoulder.

"I wonder what you have done to cause the knights to attack your town," he said under his breath.

"It wouldn't have taken much. Maybe they wanted the food reserves or supplies. They may have heard about the count's army. We are a conquered people, after all, Dar LaCross," she said with a snide tone. "We have been conquered by those soldiers that you seem to hold in such high regard." Fayette waited for a response.

"We should get some rest if we are to travel to the coast in the morning," Dar said with a coolness that could crack an egg.

"What? To the coast? Wait, you can't take me to the Baile! I can't go there!" Fayette was outraged.

"Why can't you go there? Are you a criminal?" Dar inquired innocently.

"I have to return to Eamhain. I guess Isabel and I will continue on this road alone then." Fayette began to come to a decision.

"You can't travel alone. There all sorts of dangers out there just waiting for a woman traveling alone. And what of Isabel? What is in Eamhain anyway that you would have to go there so adamantly?" Dar asked.

"My duchess is at Eamhain, and I serve her. She has to know that Teamhrach was attacked. I must return to Eamhain. I have no choice."

"You always have choices, as do I, and I cannot allow you to travel the countryside alone," Dar said with authority in his voice.

"Are you planning to drag me to the Baile against my will?"

In the small place between the soft smile on Fayette's face and the silence of her question hanging in the air, Dar came to an understanding. "Your loyalty is commendable, and I would like very much to see you to your duchess. I will protect you and pledge to get you safely to your duchess. But it is important that I meet with the knights and..."

In Fayette's head, she began to formulate the words that would make the difference between Dar helping her or not. She was certain she did not need a man to help her, let alone protect her, but the truth was plain to see: Dar had a sword, and if the soldiers who attacked the town found her and Isabel, they would not be able to protect themselves from them. As she opened her mouth, some unexpected words found their way from her lips.

"Well, the road is quite dangerous. Thank you for pledging to take us to Eamhain. You are an honorable man who wouldn't abandon two women on the road, I see that now. Anyway, I am sure the duchess will have some reward for your generosity." Fayette worked to entice Dar.

"But I..." Dar had not intended to agree to take Fayette and the girl to Eamhain, but agree he had unwittingly done. He had learned that a knight was honorable and true to his word, and because his word had agreed to take Fayette to the duchess, he now felt a pulling obligation to do so. "If I am to take you to this duchess of yours, then you should get some rest and leave at first light. It's a long journey. What about the girl? Were you planning to just drag her across the county? That seems unfair to a small child to do. Is there somewhere that we could leave her?"

"Miles, her father, told me that he would meet us at the clearing on the King's Road. Even if the soldiers leave, he will wait for his daughter to be returned. The King's Road can't be far from here. We just have to get there," Fayette explained, and she began telling Dar where the clearing was located.

Fayette walked over to where Isabel was sleeping, curled up next to her, and put her arm around the child. It had been a long day, and she had to admit that if Dar had not come along, she would still be trapped in the crevice. As she began to nod off, she looked over at Dar, who was consulting his strange and mysterious book once more. Dar looked up at the stars and then down at the page. It was beyond her what Dar was up to. The man was as much a mystery as the book. She could not even make heads or tails of why he came to Hibernia in the first place. She thought the whole story of joining Aviticus's soldiers was a bit suspect anyway.

Dar realized they could not travel with a small child, and finding Miles became a paramount purpose. He viewed the book, looking for a landmark or a star location that would tell him where he was and how to get back to where he had been, but he found nothing. He closed the book in frustration and wedged it back down in the vacant hollow of his pocket and took his bag off his back. It was starting to get chilly, and he was glad to have packed his bedroll. Untying the ropes that held it together, Dar looked across to where Fayette and Isabel were lying. They were huddled together, trying to stay warm in their sleep.

Dar walked over to the two women and covered them with the blanket and tucked it underneath so nothing would crawl in with them. Fayette was in the place between worlds when she awoke to the touch of Dar dropping a blanket on her and Isabel, her bedfellow. She was careful not to startle as she awoke, curious about what this man was doing. She felt his hands begin to move the blanket underneath her shivering body. It was a sweet gesture she had not expected.

She was certain he would invite himself to curl up next to her, but this man, Dar, would not give in to his emotions. She watched from the corner of her eye as the strange man walked away to find comfort against a rather large rock that was neither soft nor comfortable. Who was this man, and why did he give up warmth intended for him? He asked for nothing in return yet sat opposite the two girls, keeping a watchful eye for danger and refraining himself from the comforts of a woman. This was the third time Dar had sacrificed himself for them, and he did not even know them. *Nobody does that,* she thought to herself. *It is unthinkable.*

Unaware that Fayette had awoken, he stood there for a moment, admiring what he had done, and then walked back to where he had packed his gear and, pulling his coat over himself, settled in for a long nap. Resting, he began to think about the conversation in which he had agreed to abandon his quest and bring Fayette to a city he had never heard of. Eamhain was not a city found in his book, but she was someone in need of help. In his cherished book, a knight helps those in need without concern for the cost of the duty. This was one of the main edicts of knighthood, and he felt that if he was to be a knight, it would be good for him to start to get used to following such edicts.

Several hours later, Fayette awoke to the sounds of birds singing in the trees and the smell of something cooking on an open flame. Her body ached as she rose from the hard, cold dew-covered ground where she lay during the night. She was surprised nothing had disturbed her sleep, and little Isabel was still making light snoring noises. She folded herself to stand and looked around for Dar, who was happily cooking something in a battered tin pot he had hidden in his bag of many odd things. *Oh, so he is a cook now,* she thought to herself in jest.

Fayette slowly covered Isabel with the part of the blanket she had recently occupied, as not to wake her. She walked over and sat down on the large stone Dar had slept on. It was as hard as she had imagined, yet Dar seemed jovial and pleasant.

"What is in the pot?" she asked, taking deep breaths of the aroma emitted from the boiling pot.

"I found a stream on the other side of the hill here," he said while smiling at the tired woman rubbing her eyes. "There were some leeks and berries growing next to the water."

"Well, aren't you the lucky one," she baited.

"I was thinking that if we follow the stream, it probably ends in the reservoir that you spoke of," he continued.

She looked into his overly charming face as if disgusted with something, causing Dar to stop tasting the meal he had been cooking and stare back at her. "What are you looking at?"

Fayette spoke slowly and softly, "That is poisonous."

Dar sprayed the soup out of his mouth with the force of a geyser and then looked up to see Fayette laughing as she fell backward off the stone she had been sitting on. Dar had a scalding scowl on his face as he realized he had been the butt of a joke she had made at his expense. Fayette was laughing hard enough that Dar thought she might actually hurt herself, and as he watched, his anger began to subside until he, too, began to start laughing. Soon Isabel had woken up and was standing and watching Dar and Fayette sitting at the fire, laughing together.

"What's going on?" Isabel cried out while rubbing the sleep from her eyes.

"I made breakfast," Dar answered. Isabel placed her hand on her hip and, narrowing her eyes, looked at the two giggling young adults.

"Well, I don't think that is very funny. You two are silly," Isabel replied and sat down, thinking she was missing something.

With the scolding from the little girl, they stopped laughing. Dar and Fayette just looked at each other without saying a word, but for the first time since they met, they seemed to have a meeting of the minds and then began laughing again—this time, together. Isabel folded her arms and began to pout. Dar quickly handed the little girl a bowl of the leek soup, and she immediately perked up with a smile. He then handed Fayette a similar bowl, while he began to eat out of the pot he had cooked in.

"This is surprisingly good," Fayette said. "So you were a cook then?"

Dar looked up at his inquisitor, and after consideration of his response, he simply said, "No, not a cook." He quickly shoveled a spoonful of soup into his mouth.

"Oh, well, I am appreciating that you are a good cook." She waited for a response but got none. "I will figure you out one day, Dar LaCross."

"There is not much to figure out, Fayette," Dar said with an edge. "I am but a simple man."

"I don't know. I think you are anything but simple," she replied.

After finishing their soup, Dar collected his cookware, wiped it out using a cloth from his bag, and then prepared for their journey to the stream he had found. Fayette was happy Dar had taken the time to determine how to find their way back to the coast, and she hoped to reach the reservoir before Miles had to leave.

CHAPTER 6

LONG WALK TILL SUPPER

After Dar packed all his gear, the three intrepid travelers enjoyed a moment on the serene embankment of the freshwater stream that Dar had guessed would take them to the reservoir, where Miles and Fayette's soldiers would be waiting for them.

"We should get going," Dar announced after he had filled the last of the waterskins. Dar scanned the tree line, looking for any dangers that might be lurking in the shadows, but found nothing. The birds were quiet, and there were no squirrels or rabbits to be found. This was alarming to Dar, who was expecting a dragon to pop out of the forest at any moment.

Isabel was dangling her feet in the water, while Fayette was soothing herself by dripping cold water on her face and neck with a cloth she had carried in her sleeve.

"How long should it take us to get to the reservoir?" Fayette inquired.

"Not long. We should get there by morning tomorrow at the latest," Dar answered. "We have to leave now. Something isn't right here."

Seeing the urgency on Dar's face, Fayette lifted Isabel out of the water, taking her hand, and looked to Dar for direction. He gestured to walk in the direction the stream was flowing. Dar secured his sword on his side and followed behind the two ladies so he could see in all directions. Dar and Fayette remained quiet until they had cleared the area. Soon Isabel began running ahead and collecting the small yellow flowers that grew along the stream bank.

Soon the birds began to sing again, and Dar became a little more relaxed. Fayette drifted back so she could talk to him.

"Is everything all right?" Fayette inquired, with a smile that could destroy any man's preoccupations.

"Yes, there was something…But it seems to be fine now," Dar answered hesitantly.

"What was it?"

Dar looked behind them once more but saw nothing. "I don't know. Er, you don't have dragons around here, do you? 'Cause I felt like something was stalking back there."

"We used to have dragons. They used to rule this land in the old days, but they haven't been seen in centuries. I think they died out," Fayette replied, without a thought of the concern in Dar's voice. She then turned to face him excitedly. "You don't think it was a dragon at the stream, do you? 'Cause that would be something."

"Are you a lunatic? I don't want to have to fight a dragon right now!" Dar exclaimed.

"You mean you would protect us from a dragon if you had to?" "I would, even if it meant my demise," Dar said proudly.

Fayette was stunned by his answer and remained in quiet contemplation for a time as they slowly chased the flow of the stream down through the foothills. Isabel had put flowers in her hair to form a crown around her head and was quite entertained, unaware of the conversation between the two adults.

Dar began to relax, satisfied that they were not being followed, and began to enjoy the view of the countryside. Fayette watched as he occasionally played with Isabel and admired the long views where the trees would break. She thought about how he had given up his blanket in the cold night air without her having to ask for it. She thought about him agreeing to take her to Eamhain without asking for payment of any kind. She contemplated the man, Dar LaCross, and began to wonder about the land he was from. Were all the people of Cornwall like him, or was Dar just an outcast?

Standing by the stream, Dar stared at where the trees had parted for a long time. He was looking for something that would give him a clue as to where in Hibernia he was. The only thing he was certain of was that he and his companions were lost. He had given the impression of confidence to ease the two women so that they would not worry, but inside he was an utter mess. His first time in a foreign land, and he was lost beyond belief. He was very upset with himself for having lost his way. He tried to imagine how he was going to tell Fayette that he had no idea where he was going.

"It's beautiful, isn't it?" Fayette asked, standing behind him. "The view, yes, it is," Dar answered and looked back in the direction she was looking. In the distance, in the valley below, he saw a large lake.

"That road is the King's Road. That is where we are heading." Fayette pointed it out.

Dar thought for a moment. "How long do you think it will take to get there?"

Fayette turned and looked into his eyes with a stare that pierced his very soul. "I think you are right. We should get there by the morning."

Dar looked back and began to make note of the area below. "With any luck, Isabel's father will be there."

Fayette took his hand. "I really appreciate you helping us and saving us at Teamhrach. I don't know what we would have done if you had not come along when you did. If the guards are still there with the wagon when we reach the reservoir, then they can take me the rest of the way. You can go to the Baile, as you wish."

Dar took his sword out and presented it before Fayette. "I have sworn to protect you until you are safely home, and I intend to. If your soldiers are still waiting, then I will stay with you and continue to protect you." He stood and replaced his sword back in its sheath.

Fayette was flattered. Her face went bright red. "You don't have to. I know that you have other things that you want to do."

"What kind of knight would I be if I did not see you home?" "Honestly, I don't even know," Fayette answered with a smile. The two of them continued walking. Isabel had gotten ahead of them, but Fayette could still see her. She was still collecting flowers and playing on the edge of the embankment. Fayette was starting to feel good about Dar and now regretted leaving him at the hut of the old woods woman. With the King's Road in sight, she thought nothing could go wrong.

"Tell me of your homeland, Dar. You say you have dragons there," Fayette inquired.

"Yes—" Dar had not finished his thought when suddenly he heard a noise from the forest. Dar turned and drew his sword, but it was too late.

Men with green skin charged out of the trees, yelling and screaming as if they were insane. Dar grabbed Fayette by the hand and began to run toward where Isabel had been playing. She did not see the wild men, but she heard Dar and Fayette call to her. Isabel stood and looked toward her yelling companions but could not understand what she was doing wrong that was making them yell. She looked around where she was standing but still could not see anything. In her frustration, she started crying.

Dar and Fayette were running as fast as they could to reach Isabel. Suddenly, she spotted the wild green men behind her companions. Fear took her, and she began to cry out louder. As Fayette reached her, Isabel raised her arms to be picked up. Fayette flung the little girl onto her shoulder and continued to run down the hill.

Dar noticed that the wild green men were only on one side of the stream, which had become a river, and he began to look for a way across. He calculated that they could run into the forest on the other side of the river and hide somewhere. Dar ran ahead of Fayette, who was running encumbered, and yelled for them to cross the river. Dar reached out to take Isabel, and Fayette began to walk into the water.

As Fayette entered the water, she felt that the current was stronger than she had imagined. At first, the water was at knee height; but in an instant, it had dropped to her neck, and she was washed downstream.

Dar was watching the wild green men come ever closer when Isabel yelled and pointed to draw his attention to Fayette, who was rapidly moving with the current. Dar could not believe his luck but was not ready to lose Fayette. Dar walked out into the water and put Isabel down. The water was almost to her waist.

"Can you swim?" he asked.

"No, no! I don't want to go!" Isabel panicked.

"Do you trust me?" Dar knew it was unreasonable for the little girl to really trust him, but it was a life-or-death situation and he needed to follow Fayette before she would be lost to them. The little girl nodded and clutched Dar, and into the rapids they went.

"Now no matter what, don't let go of me," Dar instructed. Isabel clasped her arms around Dar's neck and tightened the grip of her legs around his waist.

Dar and Isabel flew downstream, clinging together as the scenery zoomed by them. Having come from a maritime culture, he did know how to swim, but he feared for Fayette. Holding on to Isabel, Dar lifted his legs, for fear of running into anything. He kept a watchful eye on what they were heading toward, hoping they would avoid any obstacles that would harm them. Although he heard the screams of Fayette, he could not see her. Her screams for help reassured him that she was well, and he continued to look for her. Isabel was no longer crying but now held on to Dar with an iron grip. She looked behind them and told Dar that the wild green men were gone.

Dar and Isabel floated as the speed of the water began to slow. As the river began to bend, he could no longer hear Fayette, and her screams for help had gone away. He feared the worst. Lowering his feet to stop their travel, Dar began to wade toward the edge of the water. He placed Isabel on the far shore and began to climb out of the water. He had lost his gear somewhere, along with his sword. The small leather loop that was supposed to lock it in his scabbard was broken and hanging to one side. The river had taken all his gear. He hoped he would not need it.

"We have to go," Dar announced to the dripping girl.

"But what about Fayette? We have to find her," Isabel demanded. "And that we will. We didn't pass her, so she has to be up ahead somewhere. We need to find her quickly."

Understanding the urgency, Isabel stood up and presented herself to Dar as if she was ready to travel.

Dar was worried. His main thought was that he had to locate Fayette fast and get her out of the water. He was starting to feel cold, and Isabel was walking with her arms crossed. He was amazed that the little girl, cold and wet, understood that it was important to find their friend and had not complained. Not fully understanding the situation, Isabel looked everywhere for their lost companion as they walked.

"Not here," Isabel said while looking behind a rock. "I don't see her. Could she have gone somewhere else?"

Dar suddenly felt uncomfortable with the situation but needed extra eyes in the water. He knelt down to Isabel's level and chose his words carefully. "Fayette might be in trouble. I need you to help me look into the water for her. If she got hurt, she might not be able to tell us." The little girl seemed to understand and began scanning the water. Dar was frantic with the prospect of finding Fayette in the water, unable to communicate. His heart leaped with every log, every stone in the water. He prayed that she had not drowned.

As they searched, Dar noticed a bend in the stream up ahead. Dar knew that the water would slow there and that they would find Fayette one way or another. He stopped walking for a moment to catch his breath. It wasn't that he had overexerted, but he was overwhelmed with the fear of how he might find Fayette. He knelt down and held Isabel by her hands and spoke seriously to her.

"I am going to look ahead for Fayette. I need you to stay here until I come back," Dar explained.

"No, don't go, I am afraid!" she shouted while looking around wildly.

"It will be fine. You can stand here, and you will still see me. I have to make sure that it is safe for you." It was not a lie. If the little girl went with Dar and then saw the lifeless body of Fayette floating in the water, it would be so traumatic that it would scar her for the rest of her life, and in his mind, that was unsafe.

The little girl was thinking of the green men they had seen upstream and was sure she did not want to see them again. Looking into Dar's eyes, she reluctantly agreed.

Dar began walking along the river toward the bend. It was canvassed lightly with trees, enough so that Dar could not see the other side of where the river flowed. Horrors of Fayette's fate filled his imagination with gruesome images only his mind could manufacture. He cautiously followed the river around the bend and searched the water for her. Large boulders created a block in the water flow, which trapped an assortment of trees that had fallen over the course of time. A pool was formed where the water seemingly did not flow. He searched the pool and the rocks but did not see any sign of her.

Dar moved in closer to get a better look at the pool. He worried he would be out of Isabel's view but was driven to find Fayette. He stepped off the embankment onto a large gray boulder and then saw Fayette's shirt lying across a limb of one of the fallen trees. He cautiously stepped onto the next boulder to get closer to the shirt. He cautiously stretched out his arm to reach for the shirt when Fayette rocketed out from beneath the water of the pool. Dar was startled, lost his balance, and fell into the pool. Fayette began laughing aloud; Isabel began to run forward, having heard the cackling that could only be Fayette.

Dar waded to the edge of the pool and reached for some branches to help pull himself out. Fayette was in a frenzy of happiness, having seen that Dar had found her, and was splashing water at him.

"How did you find me?" she blurted out.

"We jumped in after you and floated downstream," Isabel said from the embankment, offering Dar a hand up.

"Where's your bag of gear?" Fayette was concerned that they now had no cookery, food, or other supplies Dar carried.

"Gone. It's all gone. I lost it to the river, and the water seldom gives back what it takes," Dar explained.

"What is that, another knight's credo?" she taunted.

"No, it isn't. I grew up in a seafaring culture, and that is the way of the sea."

Fayette waved at the onlooking Dar as he explained. "My clothes are over there, drying. Do you mind turning around?" Dar turned his back to her as she continued and stepped out of the water to get dressed. "This is freshwater, but what are we to do about food? Oh gods! Did you lose your book? Do we even know the way back?"

A sick look overtook Dar's face as he turned around to look up at the rapidly flowing water with no sign of their gear. He shoved his hands into the pockets of his coat. Relief filled his mind when his probing fingers touched the wrapping of the book he had earlier shoved in the deep crevice of his pocket. He triumphantly retrieved it and showed it to his companions.

"I can't believe you didn't look for it earlier," Fayette commented while shoving her leg into her trousers.

"I had other things on my mind," Dar defended.

Fayette, fully dressed, was eager to move on, especially knowing they had no food or supplies. They let Isabel collect flowers and small stones along the way, which kept her mind busy and not on the fact that they had not eaten in a very long time. Fayette was dreading the inevitable meltdown that comes with a hungry child.

Unbeknownst to her, as they walked, Dar had been collecting edible plants, tasting them, and shoving them into his pocket. He was concerned they would run out of steam before reaching their destination, and he did not want that. Fayette only became aware of it when, as they were talking, he handed her a tasty leaf to chew on.

"You seem like a nice person, Dar. Why would you want to go and join Aviticus's soldiers? The Caledonians are not the nicest people." Fayette was earnestly curious.

"I want to become a knight. It is my lifelong dream to serve the people of Hibernia and make something of myself," Dar replied.

"Yes, you have said that. I guess I don't know what a knight is and I cannot be a judge of that, but I heard you praying last night with your sword. Is it your god that is making you do this thing?"

Dar struggled to remember last night. It seemed so long ago. "Oh, I wasn't praying." Dar snickered and broke off a leek and handed it to her. "That was the knight's creed. I must swear it when I am knighted."

"But what is it that makes being a knight so great anyway?" she pressed once more.

"See, that is the important question. You see, a knight serves the common people. They are wandering soldiers who will right any injustices, fix any wrongdoing, protect those who cannot protect themselves, and whose sword will defend even the lowliest. They serve no one king but live by the highest moral standards. And that is why I want to become one," Dar explained proudly.

Fayette stared at him with disbelief. "And you believe you will find these people in the Baile?"

Dar nodded.

"Well, I have lived in Hibernia my whole life, and I have never heard of these people that you described. I don't think they exist. Except maybe in the dreams of a poor young boy who wants to become something greater than himself."

"You don't believe in the knights or me?" Dar sounded offended.

"I would love for your knights of Hibernia to exist. We need people like that in the world, we really do." Fayette began to get angry. "When my city was getting burned to the ground and my father was killed, it would have been nice to have someone show up and save him. But nobody did, and do you know why? Because they don't exist. Nobody cares about anyone, only saving their own skin. And that is the fact, Mr. Dar LaCross!"

Dar thought it would be a good idea to let her cool off for a while. He wasn't sure what that was all about, but it gave Dar an insight into what had been happening in Hibernia. Perhaps the knights did not exist, or maybe they had died out. He did not know. But if she was right, then Hibernia needed the knights more than ever, and he was going to bring them. First, he would need to find a patron in which to banner the knights behind, and then he needed to find good men who cared more for justice than their own lives. But where would he find such men? That was the question he would ponder for a long time.

As they walked toward the distant road that would lead to the reservoir, Fayette remained very quiet and did not talk much. Dar feared he might have lost her.

As they approached the King's Road, Fayette seemed to walk with a bounce in her step, as she was anticipating seeing her dear Mahj again. She recognized the area of the small bridge that they had crossed on their way to Teamhrach. *Finally, something is going right,* she thought to herself. The cobblestone road had fragments of debris of the broken lives of people fleeing from the destroyed town. As she searched the area, she saw nothing of the wagon.

"The reservoir is this way," Fayette announced and took the lead.

As they reached the clearing where she had rested with Mahj, she scanned the area cautiously. There were abandoned tents made from whatever people could grab in a hasty escape, discarded chairs and clothing, and the tracks of carts that trailed in all directions. The people of the town came here and waited, but where did they go? Dar had picked up a stick and was poking around when he spotted a small group of people camped near the embankment. He hoped they would know where the others had gone so they could follow and catch up with Miles, Isabel's father.

"We should be cautious. They are probably scavengers," Dar said. Fayette gave Dar a haughty look as she walked past him and approached the group. They were people left behind who simply had nowhere to go. They had collected what had been discarded to make their encampment. Among them was Lady Fulcrum, who had gotten separated from her husband. She had been organizing a few of the maids also left behind to gather supplies discarded by the fleeing masses. She looked at Fayette with a discriminating glare, for Fayette looked very different than she had before.

"Have you seen the wagon? Lady Mahj's wagon?" Fayette inquired.

"Yes, they were the first to leave. She and a bunch of soldiers went to alert the duchess of the attack. Most o' the men went with her," she explained. "Left us without a howdy-do! Right rude if'n you ask me." When Isabel saw Lady Fulcrum, she ran to her and wrapped her arms around her waist.

Fayette snickered at the precious creature. "Is Miles here? We have Isabel for him."

"Nah, he asked me to stay here 'case you showed up. He was 'kin you might have went elsewhere, so is he went to find ya," the head maid explained. "I can take the little cherub for ya. I'm right positive he will be along soon seein you be here and not there."

"Is that all right with you, Isabel?" Fayette asked with hesitance. "Oh, yeah, she's my *noni*. I can stay here and wait for my daddy,"

Isabel said.

"Do you know who it was?" Dar interrupted.

"Who what was, deary?" Lady Fulcrum asked.

"Who attacked you?" Dar pressed.

"Coulda been anyone. My 'kin was that it being Aviticus and his group o' thugs. The young count had refused his tax men 'cause they wanted to take all the cows and leave us to starve. He threw them out, and then we all got burned out," Lady Fulcrum explained.

"And did the count go with Mahj?" Fayette inquired.

"Nah, he disappeared during the fire. It's my 'kin that he's dead," she replied.

"How horrible!"

"It's fine. It's the way of things, my dear. You best get used to it. Have you eaten? We have some food and supplies here. It ain't much but yous welcome to whats he got," she said.

"Thank you, no. We have enough," Dar said while staring at Fayette. "We need to get going," he announced.

As they turned to leave, Isabel ran after Fayette and wrapped her arms around the young lady and followed by giving Dar a hug that seemed to last an eternity. "Thank you for saving me and bringing me back to Noni," she said and then returned to Lady Fulcrum. They waved as Dar and Fayette walked back to the road for the long journey to the castle of the duchess.

"Why wouldn't you accept their hospitality?" Fayette asked Dar while they walked away.

"Fayette, they have nothing. Barely enough in that pot to feed them, let alone give anything to us. How fair would that be?" Dar asked rhetorically.

As they reached the road and began the long, hard journey, Fayette was satisfied she had brought Isabel somewhere safe, with people who would take care of her until her father returned to get her. She looked at Dar walking next to her, true and confident that he would get her safely to Eamhain, where she would once again see Mahj. But the countryside was dangerous, and Dar, without his sword to protect them, was now as vulnerable as she was. She hoped they could overcome what dangers might lie ahead on the long journey home.

There was not much to find to eat along the King's Road, and the cobbles were beginning to hurt Dar's feet. It was an old trade road used by farmers and tradesmen to move their wares to the towns and cities, and Dar was not enjoying the pastoral view. They had spotted smoke among the rolling hills that could only mean one thing: a farm village was out there. Dar reached into his pocket and handed Fayette the last of the edible plants he had gathered on the walk.

"We are going to need food. Do you know anyone who lives in these parts?" Dar inquired, with concern in his tone.

"No, but if we find a farm, they will help us," Fayette pointed out confidently.

"What say we cut across this field and find that village and meet some of those farmers who will help us out and give us supplies?" Dar asked flippantly.

Dar didn't have much faith that they would find someone who would just give them what they needed, but Dar was more than willing to work for what supplies they needed that would get them to where they needed to go.

The field looked like it was well taken care of. Nothing seemed to be overgrown. It was late in the day, so nobody was working the field at the moment. Dar imagined they were all tucked away in their little houses, enjoying supper with their families. Typical of any farm you would find, the fields surrounded the village where the workers lived. Rows of the food were laid out in a way, as if the rows were rays stretching from the sun, with the village at its center.

The crossing of the fields was relatively easy; it had not rained in a couple of days, so the ground was dry. There was an old rotted cart that had one of its wheels sunken into the soft earth, the barns were old and rustic but still in use, and piles of grain peppered the area around the farm.

As Fayette and Dar approached one of the houses, a woman came out with a basket. Fayette waved to get her attention so that she would not be startled by strangers approaching. Dar watched with interest as she did something interesting. She looked back toward the house and shook her head. She then went back into the house.

Dar thought the actions of the farm woman were interesting, but he continued to walk on. Fayette leaned over and grabbed his arm to stop his stride. She pulled Dar back into the field, where they could be concealed.

"Something's not right here. We should leave," Fayette whispered.

"If something is wrong, we should check it out. They might need our help," Dar said.

"What are you talking about? We need to go," she insisted. "Look, these people might be in trouble, and if that is the case, they will need our help. We can't just leave them," Dar said, and he began to sneak up to the house for a better look.

Fayette followed Dar closely as they made their way up to the house so they would not be seen. They first ducked behind a stack of straw in the middle of the clearing. Dar peeked out but saw nobody walking around, so he told Fayette to stay where she was. He ran to the house where the woman had waved them off. Looking around, he found an old box he could use to stand on. Carefully, he leaned it against the wall of the house and looked around to be sure no one was around. He carefully raised his head to look in the window to see what was happening on the inside.

The inside of the house was in better shape than Dar would have imagined for a farm. Sheer curtains were draped across the windows, which interfered with his vision, and he hoped it would also help his probing gaze go unnoticed. From his vantage point, he could clearly see the woman they saw outside walking around. She was bringing bread to someone he could not see. He placed his fingers on the windowsill to get a better grip on it and began to shuffle the box under him so he could get a better view. Under his feet, the old box began to crack as the weight of his body shifted it back and forth. He stretched his body to look into the house once more.

Dar bent his torso while hanging on either side of the window as he looked to see who was in the room. Suddenly, the box supporting his weight let out a loud crack and collapsed under his weight. He instinctually grabbed on to the side of the building, but to his surprise, he did not fall. Dar looked down just beyond his feet and saw Fayette standing there, holding him up. She had not waited by the straw after all. He rolled his eyes and continued his probe into the house. He adjusted his stance and peered into where the table was located. Sitting at the head of the table was a large man wearing armor. A helmet with horns on it sat on the table beside him. Dar ducked back to be sure he would not to be seen.

Having seen that the family was being held captive, Dar gestured for Fayette to lower him to the ground so that he and Fayette could make a plan. With both feet on the ground, they sneaked back to the large stack of straw.

"I could see the matron of the house, but I cannot see anyone else. Do you know how many people live here?" Dar inquired.

Fayette glared at him. "How would I know who lives here? Just because I live in the Marche does not mean I know everyone who does."

"I was just asking a question. You seem to be dressed like them. Can you go in there and see what we are dealing with?" Dar requested.

"That's your great plan? To just walk in there and look around?" Fayette was in a mood. "We need to leave and find someone who is better equipped for this sort of thing."

"We can't just leave them." Dar's brain started running in high gear to develop a plan. Dar turned toward the house and scurried over to the barn. The main door was open. Going inside, he looked around for a weapon or something he could use as a weapon to repel the soldiers from the house. The soldiers had done a good job of isolating any farm tool that could be used as a weapon, leaving Dar with nothing to find. After several minutes, his search only revealed a lock used for the chicken cages, a broken handle from an old tool, and wheat, which the barn was used to store. Dar became very frustrated and began thinking that maybe Fayette was right.

After seeing Dar disappear into the barn, Fayette patiently waited, her feet in the cold mud, for Dar's big plan. Suddenly, a soldier came out of the house. He stood in the clearing where Dar would have to exit the barn. She jumped from foot to foot, flailing her hands about, trying to get Dar's attention, but he was too wrapped up in what he was doing to notice. As Dar toiled away, hoping to find some answer to challenging trained soldiers with no weapons, the soldier caught a glimpse of something moving in the barn and, holding a cup in one hand and a plate in the other, moved closer to the barn. Just then, in an instant, Dar exploded from the barn opening and clubbed the soldier with his stick, knocking him to the ground. In a single movement, the soldier drew his sword and sliced up and across, slicing Dar's stick in two pieces, forcing him to step back from where he lay in the dirt.

The soldier leaped to his feet and challenged Dar with a sinister laugh that made Dar's skin crawl. Although the soldier was only as tall as Dar, his sheer bulk seemed to dwarf him. To avoid the heavy volitant blade, Dar weaved back and forth in resemblance to the movement of the sea. Fayette found Dar's movements quite beautiful until he began to throw the broken sticks and anything else he could find at the advancing soldier.

Fayette spotted a large iron lock, one of the many things Dar had tossed out, lying on the ground behind the soldier. Careful not to be seen, Fayette ran over to the lock and tied it to the end of the sash that held her shirt together and began to twirl it over her head. Once the lock had picked up enough speed, she let it fly in the direction of the soldier. The lock hit him on the back of the head, causing him to collapse on the ground like a sack of potatoes.

Dar ran over to search the soldier while Fayette looked to see if anyone had heard the noise, but nobody had been alerted to the brief battle. When Fayette looked back to see what Dar was doing, she could not believe her eyes.

"What are you doing? Just grab his sword," Fayette demanded with the force of a whisper.

Dar looked up to see her face and picked up the soldier's sword from the ground. It was heavy in Dar's hand, but after a couple of practice swings, he bolted through the door of the house. Shaking her head, Fayette grabbed her menacing lock off the body of the unconscious soldier and charged into the house after him.

Like a raging bull, Dar had charged into the house and tackled the soldier who was sitting at the table to the ground before he could reach his sword. Picking up a water pitcher, Dar hit the soldier over the head and knocked him out. Just then, he noticed two others storm in from the other room. Dar leaped up and made a run into the first soldier, locking their swords together. The soldier lifted Dar up off the ground and turned him so his back was facing the other soldier. Fayette now had a clear shot at the first soldier and launched the iron lock at his head, knocking him out. As he collapsed onto the floor, Fayette ran over to retrieve the iron lock from the unconscious body.

Dar turned and parried the first blow of the other soldier. The soldier leaped back and lunged at Dar's advance, but he was quick to spin to one side, leaving the soldier open for Dar's next move. Dar grabbed the soldier's hand, bent it backward, and leaped over his head, jerking the soldier down to the floor. He then scanned the room for something heavy and hit him with it.

Dar was very pleased with himself and sashayed over to where Fayette was standing. Dar was very focused on Fayette, so much that he failed to notice that the soldier had gotten up and was standing behind him, at the ready to chop him down. As Dar was smiling and about to begin a moment of bragging, Fayette began to spin the iron lock and smacked the risen soldier between the eyes, knocking him to the ground.

"Why didn't you kill them?" Fayette asked.

"It was not necessary to have to kill them. I try to avoid it at all costs," Dar replied. The truth was that Dar had worked to become a good swordsman so that he would not have to kill anyone, and as skill would have it, Dar had never killed anyone in his life. Even the stray dragon back in his home of Cornwall was given quarter to retreat to its lair.

The family of the house rushed to Dar and Fayette and thanked them both. They would bring the soldiers to one of the barns and tie them up. The village would then keep them healthy and fed until the duchess's men would arrive and take charge of the prisoners properly. The farmers were only too happy to serve Dar and Fayette a well-earned meal and to give them the supplies they needed for the journey back to the castle.

CHAPTER 7

THE KNIGHT RISES

Dar and Fayette were soon on the road again. Fayette, having seen Dar in action, had a newfound respect for him and was now feeling confident in getting to the castle safely. Dar was walking behind Fayette, two new waterskins over his shoulder and the shiny new sword he had taken from the soldier at the farm by his side, feeling like nothing else should happen to them now that they had picked up their pace. The road was the most direct route to the castle, and they were making some distance between where they had to go and where they had been.

As they walked, Dar began reading excerpts from his book to Fayette, with hopes that she would understand the importance of becoming a knight. But Dar still had questions whose answers were not found in his book—answers that would have to come from a local source.

"When we were in the hills and were attacked by those green men... er, what were they?" Dar asked. "I have never seen anything like them."

"They are the Ork. They are an ancient tribe that lives in the broken lands. They say that they paint their bodies with absinthe, a plant found in the Angriis, which makes them twisted and insane. Nobody knows for sure, because anyone who has sought them out has never returned," Fayette explained. "The absinthe has made them more monsters than men."

"They sound dangerous. We will have to make sure we don't run into them again," Dar replied.

"They hardly ever come down from the broken lands." "That sounds comforting," Dar said sarcastically.

"I am sure you could handle whatever will come our way," Fayette said earnestly.

After seeing Dar in action at the farmhouse, she was sure things were going to be all right. The chore of getting to the castle just got a little easier in her mind. Dar had practiced long and hard to become an expert swordsman, but he was still uneasy about fighting with the sword. Swords kill people, and Dar was a bit too sensitive to take a life. Realizing now that Hibernia was the wilderness he was told it was, he started to wonder if he was really up to the task of becoming a knight after all.

"Are you feeling unwell? You don't look good at all," Fayette asked, looking at his pale complexion. Concerned for him, she brushed the back of her hand against his cheek while she waited for him to answer.

Full of self-doubt, he considered his answer carefully. *A knight is truthful,* he thought to himself. "We got lucky back there. I am afraid that if we stay on the road, we will get attacked again. Do you know a better way to get to the castle?"

"This is the best way to go. This road is patrolled, so I am sure we won't run into any more trouble," she said confidently.

"Patrolled by whom?" Dar inquired.

"Well, that is complicated," she began. "Many years ago, an army from Caledonia led by a warlord named Aviticus. Crossing over into Darini, he captured the kingdom of Eamhain and then Manapii, where he set up his kingdom in the Baile. His will is the law now."

"That must be why nothing matches with my book. It must be a chronicle of the time before the invasion," Dar interrupted.

Fayette continued, "His soldiers now patrol the old roads and have toll outposts where they collect goods from people using the roads and bridges."

"You only pay taxes in the form of tolls?" Dar asked.

"Not just. They occasionally show up at the towns and villages to collect what they call taxes. They take food and supplies sometimes, leaving nothing for the people they take from," Fayette answered with disdain.

"Doesn't sound fair to me," Dar said while staring into the distance.

"The duchess compensates the farmers when she can," she replied.

Dar turned to Fayette and said with true enthusiasm in his voice, "I look forward to meeting this duchess. How far do we have yet to go?"

"I am guessing that it will take a full day to get there from here," Fayette reckoned.

The King's Road was the safest route, but it was not regularly patrolled as Fayette believed. For the most part, the tolls were harmless, taking a random chicken or the occasional cow, and never caused anyone any real harm. At least, that was the consensus that the duchess did not abide but had no recourse to change. She simply waited for opportunities to change such things for her people.

As they approached the toll bridge, there was a line of refugees and carts of all shapes and sizes lined along the road, with people waiting. Fayette started craning her neck, looking for the large black wagon that would be carrying Mahj, but it was not on the road. As they walked past the many farmers and families waiting to cross the bridge, the people all stared and wondered who they were that they did not have to wait like the rest of them.

"Hey, the queue starts back there!" a man yelled out while they passed. Fayette had stopped, but Dar gently took her arm and continued on to the bridge.

Fayette and Dar reached a place near where the traffic block was, but they still could not see what was causing the problem. Determined to find out what the trouble was, Fayette climbed on top of one of the carts that were parked on the road. She was able to see in the distance three soldiers wearing the black armor of Caledonia standing on the bridge while yelling at an old man who was frantically trying to get his mule to stand up.

"I am sorry, me lord, I don't know what to do. She saw you waving your sword about, got frightened, and she won't get up," the old man cried.

"Move this animal, or I will move it for you," the soldier said while drawing his sword.

"No, me lord! She is all I have. She is just bit upset. Just stand back, and I will get her off the bridge," the old man pleaded, placing himself between the mule and the soldier.

"I claim your cart and goods in the name of Aviticus! Get this man off of my bridge," the sergeant barked to the other two soldiers, who forcibly took the old man from in front of the mule so that the sergeant could slay the stubborn beast. "We will be eating meat tonight, boys!"

Fayette went to tell Dar what she had seen and to let him know they should not get involved, for the men in the black armor were the law imposed by their warlord. When she looked down, he was already on his way to the bridge. Fayette could only imagine what trouble he was about to start when she, in a panic, jumped off the cart to run after him.

"Dar! No!" she cried out. Dar had stopped and turned toward Fayette, who grabbed his arm, with a questioning look on his face. "These men belong to Aviticus's army. We cannot get involved." Dar looked into her face, deep and thoughtful, considering what she told him.

"I know men like this. An imperial army came to Cornwall many years ago. They conquered our lands because they were many and we were few, but we never gave in, never gave up. After capturing our capital, they had established a city nearby and claimed our lands. We found other means of resistance. We cannot allow this sort of thing to go unchecked. Somebody has to do something," Dar belabored.

"Why does it have to be you?" Fayette pleaded.

"If not me, who then?"

As the words hung in the air, Dar turned and ran toward the bridge to help the old man. He ran like a shot, drawing his sword; everyone got out of the young warrior's path until he reached the mule unnoticed by the sergeant about to cut down the disobedient ass. Dar ran up and blocked the killing sword blow of the sergeant with his sword, saving the mule from its fate. He quickly put the point toward the soldier's chest and demanded he stop what he was doing.

"Who are you to demand anything of me?" the soldier asked.

"I am Dar LaCross! This man has done no wrong. If you allow me, I can get the animal to move and clear the bridge," he announced.

"Seize this man and get him off of my bridge," the sergeant ordered the other two soldiers once more. They threw the old man on the road, and then they approached Dar, drawing their swords. Dar would not have this and shifted his stance to defend himself.

The soldiers saw Dar's dress and prepared themselves for a short duel with an untrained swordsman, but they were unprepared for what Dar was about to do to them. The eager soldier lunged at Dar as he spun around, locking his blade with his and quickly disarming him. Dar then leaped up and kicked the man in the chest, knocking him off the bridge and into the mud-lined embankment below.

The other soldier hesitated for a moment and then charged Dar. Once again, he became a whirling dust cloud of blades, blocking every attack the man had. Dar finally used the man's own momentum and pushed him over the railing of the bridge, making him land next to his partner in the mud below. The crowd cheered as Dar turned his sword toward the sergeant, who seemed reluctant to fight the young swordsman.

"You tell this Aviticus of yours that this land does not belong to him! This is the land of the duchess of Eamhain! Tyranny will no longer be tolerated here," Dar challenged the sergeant, but his challenge would go unmet.

The sergeant retreated from the bridge as he collected his two soldiers from the mud and quickly ran off. Dar then sheathed his sword and turned to the mule. His face appeared more gentle, and his body more docile. He leaned into the face of the mule and seemed to whisper in its ear. Nobody would ever know what Dar said to the mule, and he would never say; but the stubborn animal found it in her to stand up and move from the bridge on her own. The mule walked over to the old man, who was in shock of what the young man was able to do.

"Who is that man?" a woman asked Fayette, leaning down from the height of her cart.

"That man,"—she snickered—"that is the knight of Hibernia," Fayette answered, without a thought of what she might be saying.

"Not sure I ever heard of that, but okay," the woman replied. Dar stood up on the railing of the bridge so that everyone would hear and began to address them. "People of Hibernia, you no longer have to labor for a king that does not care for you. Do not cater to soldiers who would take and leave your family with nothing. Don't fear these monsters that would kill your only mule for their pleasure. I am heading to see the duchess of Eamhain now, and I make this promise to you that I will do all in my power to stop this! Join me, and together we will save Hibernia from this tyranny."

They were great words, but they did not get the response Dar was hoping for. Once the offending mule was moved from the bridge, the traffic began to move across once more. The farmers and traders passed and smiled at the strange man, never saying a word of thanks to him.

For the moment, the stories Dar had been mentioning to Fayette about a mysterious group of soldiers who would come to save the people of Hibernia seemed to be true in the actions of this one man. It appeared to the people on the road that day that a knight of a greater mission had arrived and that man was sworn into service to protect Fayette. For the first time since he had said the words to her, it started to mean something. She started to wonder if this man could be the key to liberating their bondage from the warlord Aviticus.

"You know there will be trouble for what you just did," Fayette scolded.

"I could not, in good conscience, allow that man to do what he was doing," Dar answered.

"Why not? It was not our business to get involved. Why did you?" Fayette asked.

Dar looked at her as if trying to see into her brain. "Don't you understand? Evil acts beget evil, and those who stand around and watch without doing anything to help are complicit in that same evil."

Fayette struggled to understand. "Do you mean to tell me that because I did not protect the old man from that soldier, that armed soldier, I would have also been guilty of beating and killing his mule?" Dar turned to her. "Yes, you would have been. And so would everyone else who stood by and watched."

"The farmers? They were just unarmed farmers. What could you expect them to do?" Fayette asked flippantly.

Dar became thoughtful until a moment of clarity appeared on his face. "They could have joined hands and stood together to build a human barrier between the old man and the soldier." Fayette could not believe what she was hearing as her mouth dropped open. "Don't you understand? If you allow injustice to go on unblocked, it will not end. Do you think that if I had not stepped up, it would have ended with an old man and his mule?" Dar asked.

Fayette did not have an answer for Dar because in her heart, she knew that the old man and his mule were not even the beginning. This was happening all the time throughout the Marche, and she knew that once the war Aviticus was fighting on the far side of Hibernia was over, it would only be a matter of time before his armies once again marched on Eamhain.

Fayette thought about what Dar had said about Cornwall, and she began to think about farmers repelling soldiers. *Could it be possible to resist Aviticus and his army?* she wondered. *Could Dar LaCross be the key to liberating the Marche and gaining our freedom?*

"I think my duchess would like very much to hear of your Cornwall and how you rebelled against your invaders," Fayette said, hoping for a creative response.

"I would like that. If I am to be a knight, I still would need a patron. Perhaps your duchess would be that patron for me?" Dar said.

"Would you help us regain our freedom against Caledonia?" she asked. The words sounded more than a mere question to Dar, and he considered the gravity of his answer.

"If I am accepted by your duchess, I will tell her how Cornwall resisted and earned our freedom. I will help Hibernia become as it is written in my book. However, before I can do any of that, I have pledged to bring you to your home safely. That is my first duty."

Fayette's face went red as the words entered her ears and tickled her heart. No one had ever committed to her so completely in her life. No one had ever spoken to her like Dar spoke to her on this day. As they walked along the road, a smile appeared across her face—a smile so permanent that she would glow for hours until sheer exhaustion would cause her glow to dim to a mild warmth.

CHAPTER 8

THE LABYRINTH

Fayette and Dar had been walking for several hours before they realized that the caravan of carts had turned off and gone their separate ways, leaving them, once again, alone on the road. It was a serene day, which was turning to twilight. Dar started to have that same feeling that he was being followed by some lurking presence, but every time he turned around to look, there was nothing. Fayette thought he was being a bit paranoid, but the quiet of the road gave her an uneasy feeling too. It was starting to rain, and Dar wanted to stop at the forest where the river forked and wait it out. He thought this would make it easier to cross the ford so they could continue on the road.

Once they reached the protective canopy of the trees, the uneasy feeling Dar was feeling began to slowly erode in the gentle sounds of the rain. Fayette pulled out snacks from her pack for them to munch on while they sat comfortably to wait. As they sat, Fayette explained to Dar that they were on the edge of the Marche, the territory that belonged to the duchess. Right across the forest lay the borderlands to the Angriis, where the wild green men lived.

"We should be fine as long as we don't venture too far into their territory," Fayette remarked.

"Why don't you just go in there with a group of soldiers and ferret them out? Then you could relocate them in separate secure areas that could be contained, and then they won't attack anyone," Dar asked.

"I know this might be hard to believe, but their number far outweighs any other kingdom in the land. At any rate, they are the indigenous people of Hibernia. It would just be bad form to attack or relocate them," Fayette argued. "You have to honor that this was once their land and that we are all just second thoughts."

While they were resting, Dar suddenly heard voices. He stood up to see where the voices were coming from, but the rain made it hard to see. He spotted five figures walking toward them on the road. They were large, like soldiers, with the swagger of men weary from a long walk. The rain made everything appear black, so it was difficult to see if they were wearing the uniform of the guard of Aviticus, who would by now be searching for them. As they drew near, one from the group spotted Dar and pointed him out to the others. It appeared to be one of the men they had foiled at the farmhouse. Dar turned with haste to roust Fayette from her resting place.

"We have to leave! Grab what you can! We have to go into the forest," Dar instructed.

"What is it?" Fayette inquired while gathering the supplies she carried.

"Could be the soldiers from the bridge, but I saw one of the soldiers from the farmhouse. They must have overpowered the farmers we left them with and escaped," he explained.

"But there are dangers untold in this forest. We can't just—" Fayette began.

"All right then," Dar interrupted, and he drew his sword to fight the approaching men.

Fayette, who was gathering their supplies, grabbed Dar's arm and just said no to him with a soulful gaze. He quickly replaced his sword in its scabbard and grabbed the remaining supplies from the ground, along with Fayette's hand, and fled into the forest. Fayette was pretty sure that they would not follow them into the forest and that they would be safe. Well, as safe as they could be among what lurked in the Uiscebeatha Forest.

The Uiscebeatha Forest was a refuge for thieves and outlaws completely unsuitable for civilized life. There were no paths or visible ways through or in the forest. The llair of the outlaw band was a complete mystery, as were any creatures that dwelled in the forest.

The river cut right through the middle of the woods, and Dar figured that if they could find it and cross, they could continue to the castle with little to no trouble. Hoping for refuge, they made their way into the forest. Dar could hear that some of the soldiers were following them in the woods. The woods were old and scraggly, with branches and massive roots in every direction. Dar noted that the very features that made the woods a good place to hide also made it hard to navigate. This assured him that the soldiers would soon get tired of following them and give up.

They quickly came upon the river. It was still raining. The banks of the river were swelling, which would make it difficult and dangerous to cross. Dar scanned the river for a way across as they followed it upstream, leading away from where he thought the soldiers would be. Deeper into the forest they went, but still they found no way across the river. Dar was searching upstream as they walked along the embankment when he saw in the distance a set of stones dotted from one side to the other across the river.

"Njihove skladbe gredo v to smer," they heard in the distance from the tracker guiding their pursuers. It was a language neither of them had ever heard before.

"We need to cross here." Dar ushered Fayette toward where he saw the large stones.

Fayette looked back to see the soldiers coming in their direction, and she stepped on the first stone. Water, black as night, was rushing underneath her feet. The rocks vibrated with the roar of the rushing water, and she became too afraid to move. The gap between the rocks was wider than she had expected, and she was afraid of falling into the water again. Noticing she was stunned, Dar stepped onto the stone and held her for a moment, wrapping his arms around her waist and caressing her back. Stepping out, he leaped onto the next stone. He turned and extended his hand to Fayette, urging her to take it and follow, but she only stood there staring at the blackness of the rushing water.

Dar began to realize that Fayette would not be able to leap across the gap, and with the soldiers coming, he had to do something fast. Dar leaped back to the stone where Fayette was standing petrified with fear, and he held her once more.

"We have to do this," Dar whispered.

"I know," she replied.

Dar held her by the waist and looked deep into her eyes. She nodded, acknowledging that she was ready, and then wrapped her arms around Dar's neck. Dar stepped out over the gap and lifted Fayette in the air, and they leaped together. Fearing she would fall, Fayette pressed her body against Dar. He had never been this close to a woman before and could feel every contour of her body as he held her close. Together they leaped from stone to stone until they reached the other side of the river.

Once they were safely standing on the far embankment, Dar began to let Fayette go, releasing his grip. Expecting her to do the same, he was surprised when she lingered just a little longer. Looking into his eyes, she began to feel that he really did care for her. This was a feeling she had not been accustomed to. Dar's face turned a bright red, which led to him suddenly feeling very uncomfortable.

"We have to go," he whispered to her and looked across the river for their pursuers. "They will be here soon."

As Dar took Fayette by the hand, they ran into the thick of the woods, disappearing from view. In the distance, they could hear the soldiers making their way across the river. The ground was a deep-red mud, which oozed from the forest itself, giving the impression of blood running down to the river. Dar realized their footprints had been giving them away as they took flight into the forest.

Fayette was looking behind them as Dar guided her way through the thick maze of gnarled trees without an inkling of where they were going. The smell of cedar filled the air with a thick red dust that began to cover their clothes. Dar began sneezing uncontrollably, giving their position away to their pursuers.

They came upon a grove that had a massive growing tree root system out of the hillside. Hoping to find somewhere to hide, Dar began to climb the great roots to get to the top of the hill. Hand over hand, he pulled himself up onto the trees, where he found the hillcrest just above the roots. When he reached the top, he discovered the hill had a steep drop-off on the other side.

As Dar stood atop the hill, it was like a great spine that snaked along the forest floor. Dar hoped this would be enough above the red slime of the forest floor to conceal their tracks. Dar reached down to help Fayette up, grabbing her wrists. She began to step up onto the roots of the great trees. Dar pulled her up with ease as her feet stumbled, trying to find good footing. Once atop the hillcrest, she looked right and then left. Dar waited patiently for her to give him the direction on which way to go, but she really did not know. Fayette gave Dar a questioning look when he let out a deep sigh.

He took her hand to resume running along the hilltop in the direction where it looked like the forest would conceal their path, but Fayette would not go.

"Wait a moment," she requested while studying right and then left. She then pointed in the opposite direction and said, "We have to go this way."

Certain the other direction would conceal them, he insisted, "No, we need to go in this direction. What makes you think we should go in that direction anyway?"

"I just have a feeling, that's all," Fayette replied.

"A feeling? What does that mean?" Dar became flippant.

"Will you trust me? We have to go in this direction," Fayette insisted.

Realizing the soldiers would soon be near, he took Fayette's hand and ran in the direction she had indicated.

The soldiers had been tracking their footsteps with great accuracy when they reached the grove. The grove had done its job and concealed their way, and the soldiers did not know which way to follow. Soon the group was spreading out to look for a clue that would tell them which way they would need to go to follow, but their trackers found nothing. It was as if Dar and Fayette had just disappeared from the grove.

Soon the fledgling soldiers of the group began to find it hard to breathe and just wanted to find a way out of the forest. As the day began to turn to night and the forest began to get dark, they knew that if they did not find a way out of the forest quickly, they might become lost forever. The sergeant of the group had decided they should abandon the search and return the way in which they came, and the others would follow.

Dar and Fayette were unaware that the soldiers had given up their search when they were running, weaving in and out through the trees that had been secreting their fluids down the embankments of the forest spine, making the ground somewhat slippery in places. Fayette pulled Dar toward her and doubled over. She could run no more without rest. Dar understood but was concerned about being discovered by the soldiers in pursuit of them. Becoming impatient, he began pacing around to make sure they were not going to be discovered. Dar watched Fayette as she struggled to breathe, bent on one knee with her hand on her heaving breast.

"You are not going to die on me, are you?" Dar joked.

If a look could strike down a person, the look Fayette gave him would have been that look. "Were you trying to be funny? That's not funny. Why don't you give me a hand up? And we will walk for a while," she said.

"What if they catch up to us?" Dar asked.

"Do you see them anywhere? If you haven't noticed, it's getting dark. My guess is that they are probably as lost as we are and have given up their search," she revealed.

"You don't know where we are?" The surprised look on Dar's face was only seconded by the sound of panic in his voice. It was getting dark, and the path was getting harder to find. Dar began to fear getting lost and began to hop from one foot to the other. "Are you ready to go?" As the words left his mouth, Dar slipped on the cedar secretions and lost his balance. He tumbled backward and instinctually reached out for a branch or anything he could find. It was Fayette's hand he would find, and the two of them rolled down the deep side of the spine, leaving a trail of their gear on the way to the bottom.

Covered in red mud, Dar and Fayette landed in what appeared to be a marsh fed by the oozing forest. It was so black that they could not see beneath the water. Vines with small round leaves grew atop the water, floating on the surface as the smell of urine filled the air.

Fayette had landed near the edge of the marsh and stood with only one leg in the foul water. Dar was not so lucky. Having landed facedown in the water, he had been covered with red and gray mud, with vines tangled around his arms and in his hair. Fayette began laughing at the sight of him rising from the water.

Dar's feet were deep in the marsh floor as he found it hard to move. He lifted one leg to move toward the edge. But when he lifted the other, looking down at where his feet would be, he saw his shoe for just a moment, and then, in seconds, the water rushed over it, making it disappear in the murk of the marsh. Standing on one foot, Dar reached down into the water to feel around for his shoe, but it was gone. Lowering his liberated foot back into the water, he walked to the shore.

His foot covered in mud, wearing only one shoe, and smelling like a pigsty, Dar walked over toward Fayette, who had been spared the ordeal. His stride stopped when suddenly Dar heard voices. He imagined the soldiers must have found them. He ran over to Fayette, grabbing her around the waist and rolling into the high grass with her. With his mud-covered body on top of her, Dar listened to the voices.

"What if it's not them?" Fayette asked quietly.

"Sh. We can't risk it," he whispered.

Fayette watched as a droplet of mud rolled down to the end of his nose and sat there, threatening to drop on her face. She bit her lip and giggled nervously. "You stink," she whispered. Dar ignored her comment and listened to the unintelligible voices talking as they seemed to be going away.

After a moment had passed, Fayette could stand the smell no more and pushed Dar off her while she smirked at him, rolling her eyes. As Dar rolled off her, he landed on a pile of leaves. As he lay there, he felt the ground begin to give way under him. He yelled and spread his arms out to stop whatever was happening to him. The leaves began to fall, pulling him into the gap left by the absence of earth under him. As he fell, Fayette reached out and grabbed his arm to keep him from falling. Dar looked around while he dangled from Fayette's hand but could see nothing.

"What is it?" Dar asked.

"It's some kind of pit. Maybe a cave or something," Fayette yelled. She tried to pull him up, but he was too heavy. She then reached in with her other hand to try to grab his shirt, but she could not reach.

Dar realized she was not going to be able to pull him up. He looked into her straining face. "Let go," he said. A look of surprise and anger appeared on her face. Fayette got one knee up and attempted once more to pull him up. Her arm felt like it would be pulled out of its socket. "You can't. Just drop me and go on," Dar said.

"No! I am not going to lose you! Not today," Fayette insisted. She balled her body with her legs spread far apart so that she would be able to lift him from the hole, when the ground where she was bracing her feet began to collapse, and the two of them fell into the depths of the dark pit together.

CHAPTER 9

DANGERS UNTOLD

Fayette had landed on top of Dar, knocking the wind out of him. She now wondered if she should have let Dar fall after all. At least she would not be trapped in the pit trying to find a way out as well. The pit was cavernous on the inside, not like a pit at all, and the floor was not what she had expected. Dar was not moving, and it would be dark soon. She knew that if she was going to help Dar, she would need some light, and soon. She got up and began to feel her way around, looking for something to burn to light their space. As she looked around, it was puzzling that the cave just did not look like a cave at all. The walls felt smooth and rippled, and there seemed to be round pillars in the empty spaces. Leaving Dar, she ventured deeper into the void of darkness around them.

Dar woke up with a coughing fit. Feeling like he might vomit, he rolled from one side to the other and tried to sit up. There was an excruciating pain in his chest; he thought he might die. Looking at the faint outline of the glow of the hole above, he realized the sun was about to go down. He thought Fayette must have dropped him, and he began to call out for her.

"Fayette! Can you hear me?" Dar cried out.

"Yes, I can hear you. How do you feel?" Fayette called back, a voice echoing in the void of the darkness.

"Can you go back to the hill and see if you can get the fire starters and toss them down to me?" Dar asked.

"No, Dar, I'm sorry, I cannot do that," Fayette responded.

"What? What do you mean by 'no'?" Dar replied.

"I am looking for something to make a fire with," she said.

Dar was a little confused but decided to wait for Fayette to return to the opening above him with whatever she would find. He knew that she was resourceful and that she would find something with which to create some light. He was glad she wasn't trapped in the pit with him.

Dar tried to get up, but the pain in his chest was too great. He began to wonder if he had broken something in the fall and hoped that Fayette would come back soon. Dar started to look around but could not see anything past the small circle of light from the opening, which was illuminating the debris that came down when he fell through. Just what was it that he fell through? he wondered. Dar reached under him and grabbed a handful of what it was he was resting on. There were sticks, leaves, and something that felt like parchment of some kind. Parchment was common, but he had never felt anything as lightweight as this before.

Just as Dar was trying to figure out if he had fallen into some kind of trap, he suddenly heard something rustling in the darkness. He was not alone. He reached for his sword and began to relax, as it was safely tucked away in his scabbard. As much as he wanted to draw it, he was still lying on the ground and could not. Dar felt around in the debris that had fallen with him and found a stick he thought he might be able to use to get up with. He rolled to one side and pulled it out from under him. Struggling, he climbed up the stick, and soon he was on his feet. Holding on to the stick, he swiveled from one side to the other, trying to see what sort of creature was in the cave with him.

Dar heard footsteps echoing in the cave, and he turned around to face the menacing creeper and prepare to draw his sword. Suddenly, from behind him, there was a light. Dar whipped around, drawing his sword to face whatever hideous creature had come to menace him, but he was surprised to find Fayette standing there, at the end of his sword, holding a torch.

"Are you all right?" Fayette asked, surprised that Dar would turn a blade to her. "You seem a little freaked out."

"Um, I guess I was. I did not realize that you were down here with me," Dar said.

"Where else would I be? Here, let me help you." Fayette put the torch on the ground and put her arm around Dar and cradled him to a clear spot on the floor. "I will light the rest of the torches and get some light in here."

"Yeah, that would be good," Dar said before thinking. "What do you mean by 'the rest of the torches'?"

Fayette became a momentary voice in the darkness, with her torchlight bobbing around the cave like a wisp. "This is not a pit or a cave," she said.

As she started lighting the torches along the wall, light began to bathe the room, illuminating the floor where Dar was sitting. It was not dirt at all, but multicolored tile, which reflected the light from the torches. The more torches Fayette lit, the more Dar could see the reality of Hibernia's past. The tiles on the floor were deliberately placed, with its colors depicting a large ancient symbol whose meaning was lost to antiquity. The massive beams that held the walls in place were of a single piece of wood, intricately carved for the intent of beauty as well as practicality. Desks were in strategic locations where work had once been done with great frequency, and lining every wall were more books than anyone had ever seen.

"The book you carry around must have come from here. I have never seen books like this, but I thought once the torches were lit, you might know what this place was," Fayette said, smiling as she returned to where Dar was sitting hypnotized by the enormous number of books lining the walls.

"It would seem that my book might have come from here," Dar said, dazed from the vision of so many books in a world where bookmaking had become a lost art and books had been lost in history.

Fayette pointed to the arch over their head. "This is an ancient language, which I am sure is the answer to your question, but I cannot read it. Can you?"

"This must be the ancient lost library of Hibernia." Dar said the words as if they held special meaning, and for him, they were sacred.

"You say that as if you have heard of it. Nevertheless, it probably says something like that," Fayette said.

"Wait, do you know what this means? This is great news!" Dar exclaimed while trying to stand up again.

"Yes, we made a great discovery. The duchess will be very pleased if we ever get out of here," Fayette chimed in.

"No, if this is a building and not some random cave that we fell into, then there must be a way out! We just have to find it," Dar deduced.

A broad smile appeared on Fayette's face, when a loud growl from her stomach echoed through the library. Dar realized they had not eaten all day, and he was glad for the extra foodstuff they had brought. He riffled through the debris where they had fallen but did not find their extra supplies.

"Do you know where the extra supplies we brought are?" Dar asked. "Yes, I know exactly where they are," Fayette answered while lighting the remaining torches.

"That is a relief. Where are they?" Dar inquired.

"Up there, but I do have some black root left over from when you gave it to me." She offered it to Dar.

"You keep it. We should look around for the exit, and then we could find some food," he said.

Fayette acknowledged that finding a way out of this place was a great idea, and now that Dar was feeling better, she walked over to help him walk. Fayette put her arm under Dar's shoulder to steady him, and they began to walk around the large round room. Walking over to the far side of the room, they came across a railing and stairs carved from marble leading down into the bowels of the once-grand edifice. Dar thought this was a great boon for them to have found such a building and now an exit in which to leave it.

Fayette propped Dar against the railing on the top of the stairs, and she then ventured into the darkness of the floor below. Leaning over the railing, she illuminated the floor. Like the floor above, the next floor was wide and dark. Using the torch to guide her way on the steps, she ventured down farther. The light illuminated the next floor just enough to see that the lower levels of the building were underwater. The murky water of the levels below was black and deep. She feared they were trapped in the upper levels now that the waters from the swamp had seeped into the library, flooding the lower levels and blocking their way out. She started walking up the stairs to tell Dar what she had found.

Fayette's face was sullen when Dar saw her walking up the steps toward him. He thought that maybe she did not find a way out, but Dar knew there had to be away out. He was determined to find it even if she could not.

"What happened? Didn't you find the way out of here?" Dar asked.

"Oh, I sure did," she answered.

"That's great! Why such a long face?" he asked, looking at her as if for the first time.

"We must be under the swamp. All the lower levels are underwater. There is no way out," she reported.

"Let's rest here during the night, and in the morning, when we have some light, we could see if there are any windows or another way out. Don't worry, we will find a way out of this," Dar assured her.

In the corner of the room was a large hearth that had been cold for a very long time. Water beads dripped from the mantle, which leaned to one side from years of neglect. Fayette brought a stack of books with which to start a fire. They were dry, and she thought they would make excellent fire starters. Dar scolded her about the importance of books in a world that had none. Frustrated, she began breaking chairs against the stone hearth. This satisfied their need for kindling and firewood, and it made her feel better to break something. She used one of the torches to start the fire, which started slow and then turned into a warm blaze.

Dar was starting to find it easier to breathe while accompanied by the sounds of Fayette breaking more chairs. There was a large chair sitting next to the hearth, and Dar thought it might be a nice place to rest while they recovered from their ordeal. But when he walked over to it, it seemed to still be inhabited by the last occupant of the library. A human skeleton still sat warming himself by the firelight. Dar's eyes bugged out with shock as he slowly turned away and walked toward Fayette. His first thoughts were to run out of this place, but then his second thoughts reminded him he had nowhere to go. Standing like a statue, with his heart pounding, Dar watched as Fayette walked past him with a fresh pile of wood and slowly tossed it into the fire. She then turned around and saw the skeletal remains sitting in the chair. She jumped with fright and then sighed as she looked around the room with an understanding of her own reality.

"You don't suppose that we might end up like this fellow?" she asked.

"No," Dar answered abruptly and turned back toward Fayette, who was standing and staring at the remains of the person in the chair. "When the sun sheds some light in here, we will find another way out."

"What if there is no other way out?" she asked, with a glimmer of fear that he would leave in her voice.

Dar approached Fayette to hold her arms to comfort her, looking deep into her eyes, and said with a calm voice, "I will not leave you. Forget about this man. He chose his fate, and we will choose ours. We are not going to die here." The confidence in his voice was assuring.

"Will you help me move him?" she asked, assured.

"What, and touch him? Why do you want to move him anyway?" Dar asked.

"I want to sit in the chair. It looks comfortable, and I need to sleep."

"You're not going to sleep in a chair that someone died in, are you?" Dar asked, horrified.

"He doesn't need it anymore. You can ask him if you want, but I am sure he won't mind," Fayette answered.

Nervous and a little freaked out, Dar began apologizing to the skeleton as they moved it off the chair and quickly placed the remains next to the hearth. Fayette then slowly lowered her behind onto the soft cushions of the chair and began to push herself into it to rest. With a fire going in the hearth, Fayette began to get comfortable for a long nap, oblivious to Dar, who was still staring at her with disbelief.

Fayette was done with dealing with her situation and started to fall asleep. It had been a hard day, and she did not want to deal with anything else. But Dar did not share Fayette's enthusiasm for sleep. Surrounded by a treasure of books and a dead man in the corner, Dar could not imagine being able to sleep. Using the stick he had found as a crutch, he got up and wanted to explore the books along the walls. As he crossed the room, he stopped to admire several glass boxes with strange devices in them. One device looked familiar to him, but he could not remember where he had seen it. It was bronze and silver, with round edges with strange characters on it.

Dar continued to walk over to the first shelf against the far wall. The shelf had a wooden plate atop it embossed with a sickle. Having been around farmers most of his life, he knew of the symbol but not its meaning here. He took one of the books from the shelf and opened it. The language was meaningless to him, but the drawings on the page showed a system of farming he had never seen before. He inferred that the library must be a depository for the wealth of knowledge of the Hibernian people and wondered why it was hidden away like this. What could have happened that the knowledge of the existence of such a library could have gotten lost in time?

He began to think that perhaps his book was part of this collection of ancient knowledge and that maybe there was more on the knights of Hibernia. Without an inkling of what symbol he should be looking for, using the torch, he began looking around at each of the symbols on the shelves. He noticed that in places the walls were cracked, the water from the swamp had seeped in and damaged the shelves and some of the books. Moss grew on the books compromised by the seepage, and with no one to protect the vast knowledge, it was a mystery how much had been lost. As he looked around, he could feel something moving around in the darkness. He was sure it must have been Fayette keeping a sharp eye on her patient to make sure he would not get into any trouble.

Making his way around the large room, Dar came upon a shelf with two crossed swords atop its mantel and realized this must be the place where his book came from. As he looked at the shelves, there were seemingly random empty spaces where books had been. One by one, he took books off the shelves and opened them to discover the strange and forbidden knowledge of the ancients. This was his time to find the famed knights of Hibernia.

He was getting tired when he heard footsteps approach behind him. He guessed he owed Fayette an explanation and imagined her standing behind him with her arms crossed, tapping her foot in certain disapproval.

Dar turned around with an open book to show her what he had found, but it was not Fayette standing there he saw. Standing before him was a large eight-legged creature with fangs larger than his arm, heaving and dripping with saliva. Dar dropped the book and moved to draw his sword, but it hurt to lift it. He fell to the ground, dropping it. The creature pinned him and attempted to disembowel him with its fangs, but having fought large lizards, Dar knew what to do. He bucked the creature until he could get his feet under it and pushed as hard as he could, flipping the creature over. However, when Dar stood to retrieve his sword, the creature charged at him, and with its large arms, it grabbed Dar. The creature hit Dar so hard that the force knocked them both back and over the railing and onto the floor below.

Fayette woke to the sound of Dar screaming her name. *What could this crazy man have gotten himself into now?* she wondered. She pulled herself from the chair and walked over to where his sounds were coming from. As she got closer, she realized he must have fallen over the railing and must have hurt himself, or worse, he could be hanging there, waiting for her. She ran over to the railing and looked down, but she did not see Dar dangling or injured from a fall. A giant spider was atop him, trying to stab him, while Dar bobbed from side to side yelling for her.

"Get my sword!" Dar screamed repeatedly, sometimes interjecting her name.

Fayette looked around for Dar's sword or any sword. She found his sword aloft and stuck in the crack between two floor tiles. She pulled as hard as she could to get his sword out of the stone. *Why a giant spider?* she thought to herself. She hated spiders and was afraid of them. A small spider put her in the gulch. Once she got the sword out, what would she do with it? Could she hand it to him? She yanked on Dar's sword once more when she heard his voice from below.

"Fayette, my sword, please! It's going to kill me," Dar yelled while dodging the giant hooks of the spider's claws.

Fayette began to remember how Dar had saved her life when she was stuck in the gulch. How he helped the farmers and expected no reward. Then she remembered how, when she was stuck on the rocks at the river, Dar could have left her but had instead held her so that she could face her fear and cross. With a newfound strength, Fayette yanked on the stubborn sword once more. As it was let go from the stone that held it, she fell backward on her bum. Quickly she jumped to her feet and ran over to the railing to look for the way down.

"Fayette, please! My sword," Dar pleaded.

There was no time to find the stairs, and with the sword in her hand, she stood up on the edge of the railing and jumped onto the back of the giant spider. Scared out of her mind, she began stabbing the creature over and over while holding it in place between her knees. Losing her balance atop the bucking creature, she fell forward onto its back. Taking one hand to steady herself, she began to slash the creature with powerful, mighty blows that brought the spider to its knees. The giant beast, lifeless and twitching, had rolled over onto its back, but Fayette jumped on it again and resumed stabbing it.

"I think you have killed it," Dar said with a snide tone as he began to stand. But she did not stop stabbing the creature. It was as if she was in some sort of blood rage; she could not hear him. Dar jumped on the back of the creature behind Fayette and held her. Reaching out, he grabbed the hand she had been holding the sword with and whispered into her ear, "The spider is dead. You saved me."

She stopped stabbing the dead creature and turned around to face Dar. Her eyes were red, and her hands were shaking. Her skin felt cold to the touch. With his arm around her shoulders, Dar led Fayette away from the creature, but as they moved away from the hideous creature, it twitched once more. Fayette turned and whacked at it again with the sword, but this time Dar was holding her and cooled her rage.

"Don't beat the bones of the dead, my sweet chuck. That was just a twitch. See, it's not moving, just a twitch here and there. You are so brave." Fayette sat on the floor staring at the large creature, clutching Dar's sword as if it would become part of her now, and began to cry. Dropping the sword, she wrapped her arms around Dar, holding him firm.

"Brave? I was so afraid," she cried.

"And you saved me anyway. That is more bravery than I have seen. You have a lion's heart," Dar said and pulled her close.

CHAPTER 10

THE ESCAPE

After the events of the evening, Fayette resumed sitting comfortably in the cushioned chair propped in front of the fire. Now wide-awake, she watched Dar perform a strange ritual, kneeling on one leg in front of the hearth. He was cooking the legs of the spider, and this was something she would have never imagined she would ever see.

"You're not going to eat that, are you?" Fayette asked while watching Dar hold one of the spider legs over the fire.

"Yes, I am, and so are you. It's not like we have anything else to eat. You have to get your strength up, and this was a gift," he said proudly while holding up the leg.

"That's disgusting. How do you even know that is eatable?" she baited, looking for an argument so that she could storm off and not have to eat the spider.

"Have you ever tasted spider before?" He was leading her somewhere.

"No, I must say that I have never sampled giant spider."

"Then how do you know that it tastes disgusting? It could taste quite good. Spider might even become a new trend," Dar teased. "Yes, I can see it now. In every corner of the world, there will be farms where giant spiders will be raised from very small ones. Stands will be located on all trade roads for passersby to come and eat giant spider legs. Maybe you could get them cooked in some kind of gravy made from nightshade fruit just to give it a spicy tang."

"Nightshade is poison, Dar," Fayette said, looking very serious.

"Not all nightshades are poison. See, you don't know everything. Perhaps you will even like giant spider legs." Fayette was not sure whether she was going to like spider or not, but she would never admit to Dar if she did like it.

"You said I would need to keep my strength up. Have you figured a way out of here? Did the spider meat somehow imbue you with the ability to climb walls?" Fayette inquired.

"You said that the lower levels are underwater. So all we have to do is swim right out of here, and then we come up in the swamp," Dar said elated that they were not trapped.

"Uh, excuse me." Fayette raised her hand to get his attention. "I still cannot swim."

"Humph, let's see if I can find a way out, and then we will figure that one out," Dar said, noticing the look of panic on her face. "Aww, don't worry, I will not leave you in this place." He cradled Fayette with his arm, patting her on the shoulder.

Dar offered Fayette the flaky pieces of spider that he had cooked and pulled out of the outer shell. Her mind consumed with the idea of being under the water again, unaware of the current situation, she took the piece of white meat and put it in her mouth. She began chewing before she realized what she had done. Fayette twisted her face at the thought that he got her to do it and then began to taste the meat she was chewing. It was not that terrible, but it was pretty bad. When she looked up at him, Dar seemed to be waiting for her to have tasted it first. She laughed and playfully hit him.

"You better be eating this horrid thing too," she scolded.

Dar began to smile, and then, without taking his eyes off her, he took a bite of the spider. As he cringed, Fayette began to laugh and playfully pushed him. Both took turns taking exaggerated bites from their piece of the disgustingly loathsome-tasting meat of the spider. Soon they were both laughing at themselves, as well as each other. She was tired and hungry, and for some odd reason, Dar did seem charming. He took his shirt and wiped his mouth with it and told Fayette they needed to sleep, but Fayette knew she would not get any sleep with the carcass of the giant spider just fifty feet from them, reminding her that there might be more of them in the world.

"Would you tell me about your homeland? What made you come to Hibernia?" Fayette asked.

"There is not much to tell. I found this book while I was fighting a dragon, and I—"

"You were fighting a dragon? You? Oh, I did not realize that you were a dragon fighter, excuse me," Fayette interrupted.

"Fine! I would rather hear about you anyway," Dar redirected. "What do you want to know?" she answered, but not really. "May start by why you are dressed in clothing to resemble a farmer but made from cloth that is a very expensive textile. Who are you anyway?" Dar asked.

Fayette began to explain how she had never known her parents. She had been told they were killed in the war, but when she asked who they were, she would always get sent away. She explained how the duchess of the Marche, Lady Ysbeth, had raised her with other war orphans of noble families. As she spoke of her friend Mahj and the wedding that was to be, Dar listened with careful attentiveness and asked pointed questions. Fayette had never had anyone interested in her before and was taken by Dar's interest. Suddenly, Dar got up and announced that tomorrow would be a long day and that they both needed to get some sleep. It was a little abrupt, but Fayette was getting tired and she did not want to be eating the spider for another day.

Dar walked over to the other side, where a second soft chair was missing, and lay down on the floor. He looked around for somewhere to put his head where it would be soft. Fayette pulled one of the down pillows from her chair and threw it at him while he was not looking. After being hit on the side of the head, Dar picked up the pillow and turned to look at Fayette, who was giving him a gentle smile. He thanked her and placed the pillow under his head and settled down. Fayette took another bite from the spider leg and threw the remaining portion into the fire. She pushed the remaining pillows together and curled into her chair. Just as she was prepared to fall asleep, she heard a noise coming from the direction in which Dar was lying. She rolled over and placed one of the pillows over her head when she realized it was Dar, who had begun to snore.

Dar did not know how long he had been asleep, but when he awoke, he was more than ready to get out of their prison. Fayette was still sleeping when he looked around and sharply realized he had nothing to gather up. He was feeling better and was able to walk down the stair unassisted. Bracing himself on the railing, he went down to the edge of the water and dipped his feet in. He had not had a morning swim since he had left home, and he had been looking forward to it since Fayette had told him of the floodwaters the night before. Knowing that Fayette could not swim, Dar wanted to make sure there was a way out before they attempted swimming into the darkness of the library. He removed his clothes and dove in.

Fayette arose quietly after a long restful sleep. With all the dangers she had encountered in this place, she was surprised she did not suffer nightmares or restlessness. She jumped up from the chair where she slept and ran over to wake Dar, but he was gone. She called out for him, but there was no answer. Thinking that Dar might have left her, she ran downstairs to the edge of the water, where she found a pile of his clothes. *Why would he leave me without saying anything? It seems out of character for him,* she thought. She sat on the floor and picked up his shirt and smelled it. Before she knew it, she started sobbing, upset that he left her in this place just because she could not swim.

As she sat on the edge of the water, she began to get angry that Dar would leave her behind. Suddenly, he burst out of the water, spraying her as he shook his head. Fayette jumped up and placed her hands on her hips, poised for attack. When he opened his eyes, Dar smiled at Fayette, cooling her fueled anger.

"You seemed like you were sleeping well. You should come in for a swim, the water feels great," Dar said playfully.

"Why did you leave me alone here?" she demanded.

Dar could hear the hurt in her voice and spoke calmly, taking a few steps toward her, "I did not leave you. You were asleep, and I wanted to take a swim, that's all."

Fayette smiled. "Are you naked in there?"

Dar felt embarrassed for a moment and said, "Yes, you're not going to swim with your clothes on, are you?"

"I am not going to swim at all," she retorted. "Especially not with a crazy person."

"Aw, come on in, the water will make you feel better. I want to teach you how to swim," Dar explained.

"Why should I need to know how to swim? I have never even been in the water until I met you," Fayette argued.

Dar walked toward her again, water dripping from his body, and attempted to put his arm around her. "I assumed that you wanted to get out of here."

Fayette covered her eyes. "Wait! What are you doing? Put something on, will you."

Dar continued, "We both need to swim through the opening to get out of this place, and it's down there." Dar pointed in the water. "I don't know how you got away with not knowing how to swim thus far, but it is a skill that every person should know." There was a long pause before Dar said another word. Fayette was not sure if he was waiting for her to say something or if he was just thinking of what else to say. "There are stairs right here, so you can walk down into the water. Are you ready to get naked with me?" He smiled as he joked one last time.

Fayette bit her lip and said, "I am just afraid that I might drown. I almost did when we were crossing the ford and I got swept away."

Dar took her hand and looked deeply into her eyes. "I am sworn to you. I will not let anything bad happen to you. I am yours to command."

She knew from the look in his eyes that he was true. He had told her of the knight's creed that he followed, which says "A knight speaks true and acts bravely with honor," and so far, from what she could tell, all this was true about Dar. Moreover, with the apparent connection they seemed to be developing, she felt she could trust that he would take care of keeping her safe. After Dar turned to reenter the water, she began to peel her clothes off. When Dar turned around toward her, he noticed that her breasts were bound underneath her shirt.

"Why do you have your breasts bound like that?" he inquired as she began to unwrap her chest.

"The duchess wanted me to look like a boy so that I could spy on the count of Teamhrach. It didn't go well," she said.

"Oh, is that what you do for her?" he asked. He realized he was staring at her and quickly turned away again.

"No, I am more like the chief adviser to the bottle washer." She snickered. "She keeps me near to watch the gentry at court. You know, in case I notice something that she missed."

"Being adviser to the bottle washers is an important job." He wanted to say more, but just then he felt Fayette's arms around him. With the image of her naked body still fresh in his mind, now being pressed against his back, he immediately forgot what he was about to say.

Dar understood that if he could get her to kick with her feet and hold her breath for twenty minutes, he might be able to drag her through the water to get to the other side. He was worried that because she was afraid of being in the water, she might let out her breath too early. The two of them practiced for hours, playing under the water, and soon Fayette was comfortable enough to hold her breath underwater long enough to swim through the maze of the building structure. Soon Dar realized it was time to try to get Fayette to swim the whole way out of their prison. She was having so much fun that she had not realized many hours had passed, and Dar was concerned they would get too hungry to make the swim.

Dar and Fayette were bobbing on the surface of the water when he took her hands and looked deep into her eyes. "Are you ready for this?" he asked.

Fayette giggled. "Ready for what?"

"Ready to dive to the bottom and then come back up?" he asked soulfully.

"I am ready to try. What do I do if I cannot hold my breath anymore?" she asked.

"I will be holding your hand. Just tap my hand with the other hand, and we will come right back up," he explained.

"I can do that," Fayette said and began taking deep breaths. Dar watched her breathing deep for a moment and then took a deep breath, and down they went. Dar held her hand tightly as they dove deeper into the once-elegant building. They followed the marble stairs to the bottom, where there was a great art structure with bronze ribbons bowed from the bottom to the top, giving it the impression that it once spun on its axle, which came up through its center. Tapestries flowed with the water current on every wall. They swam toward what Dar imagined was the front of the building, where light was streaming in through the water. Swimming across the floor, they came across a large statue of gold. It was the image of a woman standing on an orb, holding an outstretched bow pointing toward the streams of light.

Fayette was amazed at the beauty of the forgotten building as she kicked her way past the many statues of marble in every corner. It was certainly the prize of the great king mentioned in Dar's book. Then like a flash, it dawned on her—Dar left his book behind. She pulled his hand and tapped it with the other, as was their plan. Dar turned toward her and beckoned for her to press her lips to his. Fayette, realizing he wanted to give her air, shook her head and made an open-book gesture with her hands. Dar just shook his head, took her hand once more, and continued swimming toward the light. Fayette began to think about the dedication of this man to get her out of the place where they were trapped, enough to leave his treasure behind without a second thought. There was certainly more to Dar than she had given him credit for.

The front of the subterranean building was breathtaking. Windows filled the entirety of the main wall. Light streamed from every pane of glass still intact. Bronze supports reflecting the light glowed in the darkness of the water as if luminescent. At the base of the windows were large wooden doors cracked and rotted from the ebbs of time itself. Each door was banded with bronze straps intended for beauty rather than to hold the wood together. Floating above the floor of the entrance, Fayette could see a large round symbol on the floor of the building. Suddenly, all became clear in her mind. The building had once belonged to the navigators, an organization of scholars—or wizards, no one is quite sure—who hold the secret of guiding people through impassable terrain or long distances across the sea. It was believed that they did not live in Hibernia until the conqueror Aviticus had brought them here, but before her eyes, she was faced with an ancient building that once belonged to them.

Dar began to swim at a faster pace as they passed the great gold statue and headed for the doors. The water current seemed to be passing back and forth, making it harder to swim. Fayette was looking all around, admiring the structure, when a large shadow passed over them. Fayette began to panic and alerted Dar. He looked back and saw a large fish following them. Dar turned back and swam as hard as he could toward the doors of the building. Fayette looked back once more to find the fish was gaining on them, threatening to eat her. She began to kick her feet harder and seemed to gain on Dar until they were swimming side by side.

They reached the doors of the building together. Dar was frantically looking for an open door while Fayette was struggling to open one. Dar then reached over and grabbed Fayette in the most undignified way and shoved her through an open door. Dar, behind her, swam out and began to push the door shut. As Dar held the door, the fish began to push at it. Dar gestured for Fayette to swim up and away from the fish. Holding the door as the fish was thumping it back and forth, trying to get through, Dar looked for something to brace it shut with. He reached out and grabbed what looked like a tree limb and pulled it over toward the door. He wedged it into place and then swam toward the light coming from the surface of the water.

Swimming as fast as he could, he saw Fayette swimming above him. Bubbles were streaming from her as she was losing her air. Dar began to swim faster to catch up with her. Suddenly, she stopped swimming, and her body went limp. Dar feared the worst. They were almost to the surface when he reached Fayette's unconscious body. He grabbed her waist and swam to the top. Breaking through the surface of the water, Dar gasped for breath while holding Fayette. He squeezed her tightly, and water shot from her mouth and nose as she began to start coughing. He began to chuckle, euphoric with delight that she was alive; he held her for longer than it was comfortable to do so. She opened her eyes to see Dar's face and wrapped her arms around him.

They were finally safe. Safe, until they heard voices in the distance.

"There are people over there," one voice yelled.

"Get them out of there," another voice replied.

Before they knew it, people were entering the water to get to where they were floating.

CHAPTER 11

THE BANDITS OF THE MARCHE

Bobbing on the surface of the water with a strong desire to avoid the people on the shore, Dar and Fayette scanned the edge of the water to find an alternate way out of the water. On the nearest shore was the bandit encampment. The camp consisted of six wagons, which people were living in, and several tents. The number of people now pointing the two of them out showed that the camp had been there for quite a while. Dar wondered if this was their secret home base that Fayette had spoken of. Dar considered landing on the other shores, but they were too far away for them to swim to in their condition.

"Ye come out of there right now," one of the bandits shouted.

"We can't," Fayette spoke up. "We have no clothes on."

"More the reason ye should be comin' out of the water," the bandit called to them. "I do not know where ye came from, but we ne goin' anywheres, and if ye stay in there, ye will freeze to your death." He then walked back into the encampment to wait. Others were positioning themselves on the edge of the water, waiting to see what the two strangers would do next.

It was true the bandit encampment had been nestled there in its hiding place for a long time, and they were not going to move it anytime soon. Dar listened as there was music playing and the sound of children emanating from the strange and elusive settlement.

Dar turned to Fayette and said, "I don't see that we have much of a choice. Think we should take our chances and get out of the water?"

Fayette carefully considered her limited options. She was hungry, and the water seemed like it was getting colder by the minute. The aroma of breakfast food traveled on the wind to hypnotize her nose. Dar listened as Fayette's stomach began to growl loudly. Without a word, she began to move toward the bandits' camp. Dar grabbed her arm to stop her.

"Wait, there must be another way. We have nothing. We will be at the mercy of bandits," he said.

"Look around, there is nowhere to go. We are alone here, and they are determined to just wait until we turn into a giant prune or until we dissolve into the water. Unless you have a better plan, I say we take our chances," Fayette explained.

"Fine, if that is your decision, then we will take our chances with the bandits together."

Fayette covered herself as she and Dar began walking toward the shoreline. Dar scanned the edge of the water and noticed that the man who had been talking to them had returned and was drinking from a cup. Two young women were standing with him. The bandits were all armed with swords and wore fine clothing befitting the nobility. Surprisingly, the bandits seemed very relaxed, considering that two people who just popped out of the water had just discovered their secret hideout. The two women who seemed to be waiting by the shore wrapped the shivering bodies with blankets they had been holding as Fayette and Dar emerged dripping from the water. As they had been in the water since early morning, the warmth of the dry blankets felt soothing to them both. Dar smiled and thanked them.

"Where did ye be coming from?" the bandit asked.

"We were trapped below the lake in a cave underneath the water. We fell in somewhere over on the far side," Dar replied.

Fayette seemed to be hypnotized by the smell of food and began looking around for its source. "How rude of me. Would you be liking something to eat?" asked the bandit. Fayette was pretty certain food was top of the list of things she needed with some urgency. Dar stammered to answer when Fayette chimed in.

"Yes, food would be lovely. Is that hot tea you are drinking?" she asked.

The bandit handed the cup over to Fayette, who drank it down. Her eyes rolled into the back of her head, and the warm liquid rushed down her throat, warming her body as it made its way down. The sound of rapture came from her as she handed the empty cup back to the bandit and asked for more. The bandit showed Fayette the way to the inner workings of the encampment, where food was being cooked and served by a warm fire. Dar was stunned with interest at the sounds and emotions Fayette had given away for the tea and food.

"I am called Lemont Wexler, and I guess you can say that I am the leader of this happy troop of thieves that you two have stumbled on to. Please sit and eat. Enjoy our hospitality. Cookie will take care of you, and then, when you are finished eating, I will have some questions for you," Lemont explained. He was eloquent and tended to stroke his mustache before he spoke. Rather tall and thin for a man of his stature, Lemont kept his head shaved to make himself look like a traveling merchant, but the single pearl earring he wore gave him the vague appearance of a pirate. The long sword he wore low on his hip only accentuated his style.

Fayette and Dar glanced at each other guiltily and continued to eat what morsels of food they were offered. Cookie was an old man with one eye and several missing fingers, and he loved to smile through his broken teeth. The rest of the bandits wore clothes fit for a king, yet Cookie seemed to be a happy nymph wearing the clothes he had probably worn in his youth. He lived in a wagon that had been backed up to the fire pit. It was multicolored, with its wheels well sunken into the ground, with all his pots, pans, and cooking utensils hanging from the rear, where he could get to each one.

Cookie took what looked like a chicken from the fire, grabbed a large hatchet, and cut the bird in half. He handed the first piece to Dar, who looked at it for a moment and then passed it to Fayette, who was eyeing it with intent. Fayette looked at Dar for a moment and then bit into it. After deciding that she liked it, she began eating it viciously. Dar looked around at the camp, where several chickens were walking around, scratching the ground, and chasing bugs, when Cookie handed him the second piece. Dar sniffed it and then took a bite. They did need their strength to get out of whatever situation they had found themselves in, and they had not eaten in more than a day. They were both eating whatever Cookie was giving them. After the chicken came a hunk of cornbread. It was a regular banquet.

While they were having their fill, Lemont had been watching them from the tent where he and two women lived. He stood there drinking his tea and observed their ravenous appetite. *If their story is not true,* he thought, *they seem very hungry for no real reason.* He decided to believe the two young people, and he put his cup on a log that had been cut and set on its end to be used as a table. He walked over to the fire pit where Dar and Fayette were eating and stood ominously in front of the two of them. The girl, Fayette, was pretty enough but seemed somehow familiar, he thought to himself. He wondered for a moment if he could get a good price for her in Providence, a large trading port city where pirates and traders met.

With a single gesture of Lemont's hand, Cookie, who had been very attentive, quietly left and returned to his wagon, leaving the fire unattended. Lemont took out his long sword and stuck it in the embers of the fire.

"I have sent men to locate your camp on the other side of the lake so that we may retrieve your things for you, but they have not yet returned. In the meantime, I hope that you are enjoying my generosity," Lemont said with the slick tongue of a snake.

"Thank you. You have been most kind, sir. You needn't trouble yourself about our camp. We will just make our way if we could trouble you for some clothing," Fayette asked.

"Of course, I can provide you with all that you may desire, my lady. Anything for such a beauty," Lamont said while taking a bow to Fayette. With a single gesture from him, a young woman came forward with a set of clothing for Fayette and Dar. "And just where would you be heading with such haste?"

"My brother and I were merchants, and we are traveling from Teamhrach, where we experienced some difficulties. We are on our way to Eamhain, the home of my uncle. He is expecting our arrival," Fayette lied.

"Yes, I did hear of some deeds in Teamhrach. Terrible, just terrible," he said, and he made a clicking noise with his tongue against the roof of his mouth. "We were heading to the city to sell our wares, and I would be honored if you would accompany me, my lady." Lemont kissed Fayette's hand. "The roads are treacherous and full of bandits. It would be best to not disappoint," he said while staring at Dar.

Dar and Fayette were escorted to an older tent where their many goods were stored. It was faded to gray and green, with frayed edges. As they entered the dimly lit interior, they noticed the room was lined with large wooden trunks, with clothing piled on each one. Bolts of cloth were piled three feet high to one side, with a dress dummy, male and female, on either side. It was a dressmaker's dream. The two women followed them into the tent as they were looking around.

"Lemont said that if you do not like what you were given, then you may choose from anything herein that would suit your liking," the younger of the two women said. "Will you be needing help to dress?"

"We are quite capable, but thank you," Fayette said.

The two women turned on their heels and abruptly left to wait outside the tent. Dar and Fayette quickly began to find some suitable clothing and began to get dressed. Fayette had found a dress that was appealing to her, and she laid it out. In a moment of reality, she walked over to Dar, who was looking quite worried.

"I am glad that you seem to be having a good time, but we have got to get out of here. These people are not our friends. They are dangerous," Dar said with a whisper.

"We will, but if this Wexler fellow is willing to take us to Eamhain, then what harm is there?" Fayette asked. Fayette turned and went to the other side of the tent, where she could dress without the wandering eye of Dar.

Lemont had said the roads were full of bandits, and the piles of clothing Dar was sifting through were evidence of that. It was not the stockpile of someone who would be duped easily. Dar knew that behind the smile and swagger was a ruthless villain waiting to strike, but why was he being so charming? What did Wexler want? He dug deeper in the clothing and noted that the pieces that would make the clothing valuable, the jewels, were all gone. Stored elsewhere, no doubt. Dar thought to himself, *If only I had a sword.* Suddenly, Dar heard a noise from behind him. Could this be Wexler to kill him? he wondered. Dar turned around with lightning speed to find a rabbit sitting on a large wooden chest holding his sword.

"You scared the stuffing out of me! Where did you come from?" he asked the long-eared pest.

The rabbit looked thoughtful, or at least as thoughtful as a rabbit could look, and answered, "I think we have had that conversation already."

"Is that my sword?" Dar asked as he reached out to touch it to see if it was real.

"Did you say something?" Fayette called out from across the tent. "No, I was—" The rabbit put his hand over Dar's mouth before he could finish.

"She cannot see or hear me," the rabbit interrupted and then took his hand away from Dar's mouth.

"Ah, no, Fayette. I was not talking to you," he said keenly.

The rabbit picked up Dar's sword and handed it to him. It was real enough. Dar felt the weight in his hand and waved it back and forth a few times until he sobered up. He realized that he could not have the sword here and that having it would bring him and Fayette danger. He handed the sword back to the rabbit. The rabbit looked confused but took the wayward sword again.

"You can't be here. If they find you here or me with the sword, they will kill us both. You have to leave. There will be a time when I will need my sword, but this is not it," Dar said in a whisper.

The rabbit stroked his furry face and said, "You are going to have to find a different way out of this then. Without a sword, you are at the mercy of these brigands."

"I know I will have to think of something. If only I could get close to Wexler, then I could do something," Dar said.

"You can't, but I think I might be able to." It was Fayette's voice coming from behind him. While he was talking to the rabbit, she had sneaked up behind him. Dar quickly put on the trousers he had picked up from the trunk and gestured to the rabbit that this would be a good time to leave. As they spoke, he slowly vanished with the elusive sword once more.

"How do you think you might be able to get close to him?" Dar inquired as he slowly turned to face Fayette.

Dar had never seen a woman as beautiful as Fayette in that moment he gazed upon her. She had chosen a dress similar to one she had seen Mahj wear when she wanted to impress someone. It was tight and clung in all the right places. The bodice was tight-fitting, heaving her breasts together and up into the opening that plunged from her neckline. The skirt was full and sheer but seemed to hug the curve of her hips to accentuate her figure while allowing light to fuse through, giving the impression that her legs were showing. She smiled ever so gently when Dar looked her over. For the first time in her life, she felt beautiful.

"I will get close to him, and he will tell me all his secrets," Fayette informed Dar with a soft voice he had never heard from her before. "He will bring us to Eamhain, and then the duchess will help us deal with him," she added.

Meanwhile, on the other side of the camp, Toby was very concerned about the new arrivals. He had heard of their treatment and demanded to know what Lemont's plan for them was. He had known Lemont since they were small and living in the farming village near the standing stones of Tara. They had grown up together, conning their way through their days and scavenging in the nearby ruins left by Aviticus and his soldiers, but this was the first time he was not privy to what Lemont had planned. Perhaps it was the girl he had heard about. She came up out of the water like a nymph, wearing not a stitch of clothing. Perhaps she was a water spirit who had bedazzled him.

Toby had found Lemont tying their stolen goods to one of the donkeys to bring to the market in Providence. He had been trapping all morning and was now returning with several small animals flung over his shoulder when he heard the news of the new arrivals. When Lemont saw his old friend approaching, he stopped what he was doing and turned to greet Toby with a smile and a hug.

"How goes it in the wilds?" he asked.

"Abundant." Toby was known for his one-word conversations. "I ran into the trackers that you sent to the hill. I can assure you that there is no camp up there. However, there are a lot of soldiers from Teamhrach around," Toby reported. "What are your plans for the strangers?"

Lemont was very thoughtful in his answer and could see the concern in Toby's face. He flopped a flat, round woolen beret onto his head and shoved his sword into its scabbard.

"The man doesn't speak much, but his sister says that they were heading to Eamhain from Teamhrach. I told her that we be heading there to sell our goods at the market," Lemont explained.

"I thought that we were going to Providence to sell this lot," Toby interrupted.

Lemont raised two fingers to get Toby's attention, looked around as if conspiring, and continued, "Once we get to the road, I will make an excuse to make a detour and then head to Providence. There be a man there who will give us money for the woman. As for the brother, we will deal with him in short measure."

"What if someone comes looking for them?" Toby asked while stroking his ragged beard.

"I don't believe their story about going to see their uncle in Eamhain. No one is expecting them, and no one will come looking for them. And frankly, if they are brother and sister, I will eat my hat," Lemont added.

Toby smiled. "I have some sauce for your hat when you're ready."

"Do you have the permit?" Lemont inquired.

"Yup, right here where it's safe." Toby tapped his chest, where he had a rectangle piece of silver engraved with the Providence merchant's guild seal embossed on it that he wore around his neck on a string.

The merchant's guild in the Providence was the ruling class in the city, and they protected their monopoly very carefully. It was against the law to sell anything without a permit, punishable by death. The permit was a heavy piece of silver, which everyone carrying goods into the city had to show. People coming into the city who did not have a permit would have their goods confiscated by the local authority and/ or would be arrested. The sheriff of Providence welcomed all sorts of merchants, from highwaymen, who robbed people on the roads and forests, to pirates, who menaced the seas. Those who lived under this rule were considered cosmopolitan, as they were very well-endowed in riches.

Lemont was finished checking the last of the pack animals for the journey when Fayette and Dar emerged from the supply tent. *They certainly look the part in which they are playing,* Lemont noted as he approached Fayette.

Lemont took Fayette's hand, kissed it, and smiled. "I am glad to see that you are feeling better. Sadly, I must report that we were not able to locate your camp to retrieve your things, but I have prepared an ass for you to ride on."

Lemont escorted her to a single donkey with a blanket thrown over its back. A bridle would make it easy for her to ride if she knew how. Dar helped Fayette onto the back of the animal and offered to walk the donkey for her. Soon the train was ready to make their way out of the forest. There was a path, which they used to move in and out without being noticed. In spite of it being well traveled, the path was unrecognizable as a path. Trees and grass were overgrown, giving it the impression that it was just another part of the forest, but to the trained eye, it was a clear way from the clearing of their encampment to the edge of the forest.

One by one, the bandits led the encumbered donkeys into the forest. Men with bows and swords walked all around the caravan. Dar and Fayette were instructed to follow the third donkey, which put them in the middle of where the guards walked. As they were surrounded by enemies, it was clear they would not be able to run off if they had an inkling to do so. Dar was impressed with how cool Fayette seemed, even when Lemont had ridden up next to her on his horse. Their horses were stocky ponies that only three bandits had. They were rare in Hibernia and served as a symbol of wealth in the land.

"You look very lovely, my dear," Lemont complimented her, causing her to turn crimson from head to toe. Dar looked back at Fayette and noted to himself that Fayette had somehow made herself more beautiful than she was, even without clothes.

"How long are you planning to stay in Eamhain?" she inquired while shifting her seat to give Lemont a better view.

"I only come for the market day, then I will be leaving the following day. Perhaps I will stay an extra day if you would like. Perhaps I can meet your uncle," he said while staring at her.

"We will be going right into the heart of the city then?" Fayette inquired.

Lemont was thoughtful in his tone and replied slowly, as if to examine every word, "We are going to the market. Once there, you are free to go where you go." Lemont searched her face for an indication of falsehood but found none.

Light began to stream through the leaves of the trees as they reached the edge of the forest. Lemont rode ahead to meet with scouts who had been waiting at the field on the edge of the forest. Fayette looked around but still did not recognize where they were. It was a grassy field that was not a part of any farmlands. There were goldenrod and tall grass as far as the eye could see in every direction. The caravan had stopped, giving way for the animals to graze before the long journey to the city. After a few moments, Lemont rode back to Fayette's side.

"There are soldiers along the road to Eamhain, so we are going to change direction and then camp for the night," Lemont reported.

"There are soldiers on the road? I wonder who they are looking for," Fayette said while biting her lip. *There it is,* Lemont thought. *She is hiding something.*

"Is there something you need to tell me about those soldiers?" Lemont asked.

Fayette bit her lip again and answered, "Um, yeah, well...no."

"No? Soldiers are on the roads, and you say that you have nothing to say about that. Perhaps we should just travel the road and see what it is they are looking for," Lemont said with a smile resembling the expression of a cat that just ate a fat mouse.

"No! Traveling with them would not be best. You see, my brother and I got into a bit of trouble, and they might be looking for us," Fayette revealed.

Lemont shook his head and rode back to the front of the caravan, where Toby was sitting on his horse, talking to one of the scouts. They did not want to run into a group of soldiers, for they were indeed searching for Dar and Fayette. Toby was used to this and knew many ways of avoiding such checkpoints. Hearing the thunder of Lemont's horse as he approached, he waved the scout off and sat up in his seat. His horse, although the same breed, was very different from the one Lemont rode. It was wide, with fat rolls around its tail. It resembled a large sausage with legs more than a horse. The look on Lemont's face was one of frustration as he rode up and stopped next to Toby.

"How are our guests?" Toby teased.

"The soldiers might be looking for dem. It seems that they may be fugitives after all," he reported.

Toby broke out with a belly laugh that almost caused him to roll off the back of his horse.

"So they are fine with us skirting away from the city and making camp just as you have planned?" Toby asked. "It never ceases to amaze me how you get away with the things you do. The fates must really love you. I will send someone to see what they are worth. Perhaps we may have stumbled on a fortune."

"Tell the scouts that we will meet at the usual staging area near the monastery and make camp for da night. In the morning, we'll decide whether to collect the reward here or press on to Providence. We should keep them separated so that they don't try anything funny. Keep the boy with your men, and I will take care of the woman," Lemont instructed.

"What exactly will you do with the woman?" Toby nudged Lemont, half teasing him.

"Until I get the money for the woman, she belongs to me to do with as I see fit. I will take care of her in my own way," Lemont stated and rode back into the formation of the caravan.

After a time, Lemont returned to Fayette's side. He seemed agitated about something but was not willing to talk about it.

"I have sent a scout to contact your uncle in the city to have him meet us on the road so that we won't have to chance meeting the guards who may be looking for you. We will make camp soon, and you can rest there until the morning," Lemont told Fayette as if to calm her in some way and then rode off to inform the rest of the caravan.

"We have to get out of here," Dar said in a whisper. "If his scouts come back to tell him that we have no uncle, then we are sunk."

Fayette leaned in so that no one could hear. "Once we make camp, we will escape and ride to the castle. I am sure we will be put in the same tent. Just keep your eyes open for an opportunity."

The caravan began to bend in the field to head in the southern direction, away from the soldier outpost on the road. The scouts had all ridden ahead and no longer traveled with the caravan. Although the number of bandits that stayed with the caravan began to dwindle, they were still concentrated around Fayette and Dar, leaving them with no opportunities to make their escape. Fayette was impressed with the organization and discipline the bandit crew seemed to have achieved, and Dar just wanted to get out of their situation.

By the time they had reached the place where the scouts had already been setting up tents for the night's respite, Lemont guided Fayette and

Dar to the center of the camp, where a permanent structure stood waiting. Dar wondered if this was their jail. Tents were erected to encircle the wooden building. A large lean-to was attached to the side of the building for the donkeys and horses. It soon became clear that this was a regular rest stop for the bandits. Upon entering the building, Dar was faced with the scouts drinking and gambling and a fair amount of singing. There were large hogshead barrels full of whatever they had been drinking sitting behind a bar that seemed like it had been made of whatever they could find when they built the building.

Fayette and Dar stood frozen about the spectacle when a large man with bright-red hair and a thick red beard grabbed Dar and welcomed him into their merriment. Fayette knew the man as the one Lemont referred to as Toby, and she gestured for Dar to join them. Fayette watched as Dar became inducted into the rituals known as male bonding when Lemont walked over and handed her a second cup he carried. She took it from his hand and smiled at him. Curious about what was in the cup, she took a sniff. It smelled of lavender and fermented cider.

"I can't get over how lovely you look this evening, my dear," Lemont said in the midst of the loud ruckus.

"Thank you. I saw it and just had to have it. My brother and I really appreciate your generosity. I don't know what we would have done if you hadn't found us in the water," she said.

"I am sure that you would have made do somehow. I noticed that you are not wearing any jewelry. Do you not like jewelry?" he baited.

Fayette knew Lemont must have known there wasn't any jewelry in the tent where they had gotten their clothing, but she was willing to play along. She turned to him and said, "I do like jewelry. What woman doesn't? But unless I am mistaken, there was not any jewelry in the tent that you most graciously shared with us."

"I have some really remarkable items in my tent that we will be taking to market tomorrow. Would you like to see them?" Lemont asked as his mustache twitched

"You want me to join you in your tent alone? I am a lady, Mr. Wexler. I am flattered, but I should really stay with my brother," Fayette reasoned.

"Ah, you thought that you had a choice. Look around. I am the bandit king. All I need to do is say the word, and you and your brother would be killed in a second. You know the location of our secret camp, so what makes you think that I need to keep you alive, other than to amuse me?" Lemont said in a cool voice while grinning a grin that made her feel like she was being sized up for a meal.

"Am I your prisoner?" she asked with wide doe eyes.

"Not as such. I am a generous man, but my generosity does have limits, my dear," he replied.

"I would love to join you in your tent," Fayette said, realizing that the tone of the evening just took a turn she did not count on.

The men of the scouting party were handing Dar drink after drink when he looked up to see Fayette leaving the building with Lemont holding on to her arm. She had a sick, worried look on her face as she glanced back at Dar, shaking her head to tell him not to interfere. When he stood up to follow, the man called Toby pushed him back down into his seat and handed him another drink. It became all too clear that the tone of the merriment had taken a strange turn.

Fayette was led into a large tent with faded green-and-white stripes. Lemont opened the flap, never releasing his grip on Fayette's arm. It was beginning to hurt when she was led inside. When he released his grip on her, she fell on a large pile of pillows. It seemed to her that the pretense was over. She struggled to get to her feet when Lemont, after fastening the tent door, turned toward her. She managed to get to her feet when he advanced on her. She held up a hand and stopped him.

"Have you any wine? It would help the mood," she said.

"I did bring a bottle. It's just in my trunk," he said, and he moved to a large wooden chest that, only moments ago, had been strapped to a donkey. Fayette lay on the pillows, for lack of a bed, while he searched for the bottle.

"How have you acquired all this? It all seems a bit much for a bandit," she asked.

"Oh, my dear, I am the bandit king. Many of the bandits in this area work for me. The duchess and I have an understanding," he said.

"So you know the duchess?" she asked coyly.

"Oh, yes, I know the duchess quite well. I steal from people who have far more than they should and sell it to her. What she does with it is beyond me, but it is a good system we have worked out between us. I get what I want, and she gets what she wants," Leman said, and he began pouring two glasses of wine. It was a deep-red wine that would be perfect for a man of refined taste, but for the bandit king, he seemed quite at home.

Fayette sat up and took the glass from his hand and took a sip. Fayette had only tasted wine while in the service of the duchess. Sealing a deal or finalizing a treaty would call for one glass of wine for all present. When the wine of Lemont touched her lips, she found it to be exquisite and full of flavor. For a bandit, Lemont certainly knew how to live like a king. As she sat and listened to stories of his exploits, her mind began to wander. Fayette began to wonder just what it would be like to stay with this man. He certainly desired her, and this was more attention than she was accustomed to.

She began to think about what life could be like with the right man by her side. She imagined she would marry a man of honor, someone who would put her needs before his. She would want someone who would be true to his word and protect her from dangers untold. The words Dar had spoken to her began to fill her head. *There*, she thought, *is a man of virtue.* Loyal to the bitter end, even at risk to himself. He had many opportunities to leave her, and he remained by her side, ever vigilant. Images of unspeakable acts the bandits might be doing to him began to fill her head. She knew that, with all the times he had come through for her, this time she needed to get to him.

With every passing hour, the wine reeled in her head, and she began feeling quite ill. Pale and weak, she stood up holding her mouth and walked over to the large chest the cursed wine came from. She bent over, holding one of the boards used to carry and fasten the chest to the donkey.

"Are you not well?" Lemont asked with concern.

"I had too much wine. I think I will be sick," Fayette said, gripping the board and breathing heavily.

"Here, let me get you something. I think I have some black root here," he said while digging through his bags.

Black root, she thought. Dar often chewed black root and always gave it to her. It was disgusting. But it was one of those things Dar simply loved, and he shared it with her. She gripped the board tighter while thinking of him. She thought about how he calmed her when she was frightened and could not move. He taught her how to swim when she was afraid of the water. *This is not how all this is going to end,* she thought, and as the fury rose within her, the board came loose.

"Ah, I found it. Here, just—" Lemont never had a chance to finish his sentence.

When Lemont approached Fayette with the offering to settle her stomach, she whipped her body around with the board she had been holding to steady herself and whacked him square in the middle of his face. Blood splattered the front of Fayette's dress with the breaking of Lemont's nose. Lemont wobbled for a moment as his eyes crossed, and he fell to the ground, collapsing at Fayette's feet, still holding the black root. She dropped the board and began to vomit on Lemont's unconscious body. Beginning to feel some relief, she wiped her mouth and steadied herself on the chest.

Many of the men were beginning to fall asleep as the hours passed. Dar had been tossing the cups of whatever it was they had been drinking onto the floor and pretending to drink with the men. He had not seen Lemont or Fayette for some time, and he was worried. He lifted his head and looked around the room. Even Toby, who had been keeping a close eye on him, was asleep on the floor. He knew he had to sneak out and somehow save Fayette from whatever unspeakable acts Lemont was forcing her to perform. He tiptoed out of the room, as to not wake anyone, and made his way outside. It was early in the morning, and the sun would be rising soon.

Looking around, he realized he would have to search every tent to find where they had taken Fayette. This would definitely cause him to get caught for sure. He needed a diversion so that the bandits would be busy while he searched for Fayette. The center area of the camp was encircled with torches; he had seen them when they arrived, but they had all but burned out. Dar took one out of the ground and began to look for a place to light it. Once lit, Dar planned on setting the tents on fire, which would keep the men busy.

Holding the torch in his hand, Dar ran over to the cooking cauldron, which the soldiers had made a meal with the night before. As he was stirring the embers, hoping for a spark, Toby emerged from the ramshackle tavern.

"What are you doing out here?" Toby demanded.

Dar considered making up a good story, but how would he explain the torch in his hand? *It was dark,* he thought. Maybe he needed some light. Perhaps he could even start some small talk with him and ask which one Lemont's tent was. Maybe he would even tell him. *No need to alert the guards, I was just getting some air,* he thought to himself. When the man put his hand on Dar's shoulder, asking him to return inside, Dar spun around and walloped him on the top of the head with the torch. Toby immediately folded, unconscious, at Dar's feet.

Dar leaped into action. Saving Fayette was his paramount concern. He took the torch and dug it into the spent embers of the cook fire. All he needed now was a single spark so that he could set the building ablaze. The men inside would wake to a fiery building and forget all about poor Dar, who, in the end, they would believe must have been inside as the building burned. Meanwhile, he and Fayette could make a grand escape. Moving the torch in an up-and-down motion, he was not getting a spark. Suddenly, he heard footsteps coming toward him. He steadied himself, expecting a roaming guard. With his back against the wall, he leaped out of the darkness wielding a menacing torch to find Fayette standing there.

"We have to leave now," she demanded.

Fayette grabbed Lemont's horse and led it out of the lean-to when she saw Dar fumbling with the torch in the cold fire pit.

"Are you going to goof off all night? We need to go now. Get over here and get on this horse. I assume you know how to ride this thing." Fayette was livid. Dar noticed the blood splattered across the front of her dress and decided he should do as she says. Dar mounted the horse and helped Fayette onto his lap, and together they rode off into the sunrise.

CHAPTER 12

The Duchess Of Eamhain

It had been a long day, but after getting directions from a wandering monk, they finally reached the castle of the duchess. Standing on the top of the hill that overlooked the valley that surrounded the castle, Dar and Fayette, atop the prize horse once cherished by Lemont Wexler the bandit king, stood on the road, contemplating the end of their journey.

"Where is it that we have to go from here?" Dar asked. Fayette had told Dar her home was Eamhain, but where exactly her home was, was still a mystery to him.

"We have to go to the castle just there. We need to speak with the duchess about what we have seen," she replied while pointing to the great fortress.

He scoffed a bit, as if the words had gotten stuck in his throat, and said, "Do you really think the duchess will speak with you? I mean to say, when I attempted to see the king of Cornwall to join his knights, he would not see me. What makes you think the duchess will see you?"

"She will see me," Fayette said flatly.

"Don't you think you should check in at home first? You don't think your family would be worried? We have been gone a long time," he asked.

"We need to speak with the duchess. That is how things work here," she insisted, not letting on that the only family she had lived in the castle.

Dar's home in Cornwall was also a kingdom, and he understood her urgency in informing the duchess of what had been going on within her domain, but he would have let his father know that he was safe first. He imagined it would take a long time once they reached the castle to actually speak with the duchess, but realizing that he did not know Fayette very well, he agreed to respect her wishes to take her to the castle to speak with the monarch before seeing her to her family. Knowing the duchess would probably not see her anyway and making a clicking noise with his tongue, he signaled the horse to start walking.

They made their way through the once-great city streets, where they drew the attention of the people who lived there. Very few people in the region still had horses, and they thought this person carrying Fayette must be someone of great importance. It was market day, and as they entered the town square, they were mobbed by people wishing to sell their wares to this new person who had wandered into their town. Not having any space to walk, the horse had stopped, allowing the merchants to surround them.

"Stand away, please!" Fayette yelled.

The commotion in the square soon drew the attention of the chamberlain high above the town, atop the gatehouse of the castle. Looking down, he wondered if he should send some soldiers to disperse the cluster that was by now making it impossible for anyone to pass through the market square.

"What is all this about down there?" he asked the sergeant of arms, who had also been attracted by the chaos of the crowd.

"Some person of wealth has entered the square. It doesn't look like anything important," he answered.

The chamberlain took a closer look at the crowd. "Is that a horse?" "Yes, sir. They rode in just moments ago," he said. It was hard to tell in the mob, as the rows of people began to push toward them. "You should send some men down there before someone gets hurt," the chamberlain suggested.

The sergeant had known from years of experience that suggestions from the chamberlain were usually expected to be taken as edicts rather than information to be considered. The sergeant turned to the guard standing beside him and began to issue orders to disperse the crowd, then he felt the cold, bony hand of the chamberlain on his arm.

"Is that Lady Fayette down there on the horse?" the chamberlain asked.

The sergeant looked carefully at the vortex of the chaos. While staring at the crowd, he began to think aloud, "The man I do not know, but it does seem to be Lady Fayette with him."

"Clear the rabble and take them into custody, Sergeant." The voice of the chamberlain was giving him an unmistakable order. He snapped into action and ordered his men to do as he had been told.

The merchants were not giving Dar and Fayette an opening to move in any direction. She had been trying to push them away, but more seemed to be filling the square. The head of the horse had started to jerk back and forth, but the group was too massive to allow any space. Merchants, holding their goods, wanted to be the first to sell to the wealthy stranger who had ridden into the square, but Dar was not buying. This only seemed to build the crowd into a frenzy. Suddenly, soldiers began pouring out from the gatehouse, carrying halberds to disperse the mob. The sea of merchants soon parted to allow the soldiers to reach Dar and Fayette.

"Take them into custody," the sergeant said.

The soldiers took Fayette and Dar off the horse and guided them into the gatehouse, followed by their horse. Dar did not understand what was happening when the soldiers brought them into the courtyard of the castle. Under the direction of the chamberlain, Dar was immediately ushered toward the dungeons beneath the fortress by four armed soldiers, who were poking him with the points of their halberds. Fayette began screaming when the soldiers pulled her away from him, but Dar looked back at her with a "don't worry" look just before being led into the stockade.

Dar knew they could not have broken any laws during their short stay in the town square, but as the fingertips of their outstretched hands were pulled apart from each other, Dar knew they would just have to wait, for the magistrate would release them. Unarmed and outnumbered, he did not plan to give the soldiers any reason to keep them imprisoned any longer than needed. He was only returning someone to her home after all. It was not until he heard the lock of the cell door latch that the harsh reality of his situation dawned on him. It became all too clear that he would be detained for a while.

Dar sat down on the stone shelf that had no doubt been used as a bed by many prisoners before him, and he began to wonder what kind of trouble he had gotten himself into by coming here. It was foolish to think they would get the opportunity to speak with the duchess. Just who did Fayette think she was anyway? Since Dar had come to Hibernia, he had been faced with one danger after another. He began to think that if he got out of this unscathed, it might be time to head back home. After all, there were no knights of Hibernia, and that was why he had come to this awful place. He was concerned about what would be happening to Fayette. After all this, she would have to live here and deal with what she had done. During the hours that would pass, Dar would wrestle with his mind over thoughts of leaving Fayette.

At the other end of the castle, the two guards who had removed her from Dar's side now presented Fayette to the chamberlain, who was waiting in the keep for her. His stony gaze gave very little in the way of knowing what he was thinking. He appeared stern, with his arms folded over his chest, and spoke no words to the guards. After a quick salute, the two soldiers turned and marched back to their post at the gatehouse.

"We have been very worried about you, my dear," he said in a cool monotone.

"I need to speak with Her Grace," she demanded.

"In due time, in due time. I am sure that you will want to clean up. Mahj will be pleased to see you. She reported that you were dead. The duchess will be very pleased that the rumors of your demise have been exaggerated. What is this thing you are wearing?" the chamberlain asked.

"I like it. I might start dressing like this more often. Get used to it. And what have you done with Dar?" she demanded.

"So the young man has a name. You are concerned for him?" the chamberlain asked with something that would pass as a grin on his face.

"He just brought me home safely. You should be rewarding him, not throwing him in the dungeon," she said, trying to cover her embarrassment.

"Hmm, interesting," he said while rubbing his hairless chin. Fayette followed the chamberlain to her apartment, where Mahj let out a scream and wrapped her arms around Fayette to greet her. While holding on to her, Mahj broke out into tears at the thought that she might have lost her friend.

"I was so lost without you. Don't ever scare me like that," Mahj scolded.

"Get her washed and ready. The duchess will want to see her right away," the chamberlain instructed.

Mahj took Fayette into the room and called down to the maid for hot water in which to bathe her. Mahj admired the dress she wore and offered to lay out a fresh set of clothing for Fayette to wear.

After the door had closed in his face, the chamberlain walked to the duchess's apartment, where she was still mourning the loss of Fayette. She could not bear to see anyone for days after hearing the news. The duchess threw a powder dish at the door upon the arrival of the chamberlain.

"I need to speak with you," he announced. "I have news of Lady Fayette."

The duchess, consumed with grief, ran to the door hoping to hear some good news. She flung open the door, looked up and down the hall to make sure their conversation would not be overheard, and pulled him into her room. She pushed the door closed and walked across the room to her vanity and sat down in front of the mirror.

"You had better have good news, Chamberlain. I can't take much worse," she demanded.

"Lady Fayette arrived moments ago with a young man," he informed.

The duchess leaped up from her chair before he could finish his sentence. She was beside herself and began looking from side to side uncontrollably.

"I should go to her," she said excitedly.

"No, Your Grace. You are still the duchess, and there are still dangers for her. I will bring her to you when she has cleaned up," he said.

"I thought she was dead. You told me she was dead. How could you have done that to me? I need to go to her," the duchess said.

"My people have said that she was not with the survivors. I would not have informed you of her demise lightly," the chamberlain explained.

"She is home now. I will go to her and see what happened. Nothing you can tell me is going to change my mind," the duchess said while fixing her makeup.

Fayette was in the bath when the duchess, Lady Ysbeth, walked in. She was wearing a simple classical dress and a housecoat that draped down to her ankles. Fayette had been reclining in a modest round tin tub with her eyes closed and did not notice the duchess entering the room. Lady Ysbeth tapped Mahj on the shoulder and gestured for her to quietly leave her with the wayward woman. Mahj tiptoed out of the room and closed the door to give the duchess some privacy with Fayette.

Lady Ysbeth picked up the sponge that had been floating on the surface of the bathwater and began to wash Fayette's shoulders. Thinking it was Mahj, Fayette moaned with pleasure and touched her hand with her fingertips.

"You're safe now, my sweetheart," Ysbeth said softly.

Realizing that this was not Mahj but the duchess, Fayette opened her eyes and jumped from her reclining position.

"Shh, it's all right," she said, attempting to soothe her back into her reclining position in the tub. "I am glad that you are home now. I was so worried, and I want to hear everything."

Fayette began recounting the events of her adventure since the attack on Teamhrach in detail. She told Ysbeth of how Dar had saved her many times on their journey, and she pleaded to have her release him from the dungeon. Lady Ysbeth listened with great interest, and when it was done, she dried Fayette off with a large towel hanging on the rack that stood in the corner of the room. Escorting her to her apartment, where Mahj was waiting, she tucked Fayette into her bed and sat down next to her.

"Do you have feelings for this man?" Ysbeth asked.

"No," she said flatly, shaking her head emphatically. "He is a hero and should be rewarded, not put in the stockade. Without his help, I would be dead several times over, but feelings for him, absolutely not. No." She stared into the distant memory where she and Dar were together.

"I will see to the young man and make sure he gets what he deserves. You rest now and get some sleep. You had quite an ordeal," Ysbeth said, and she kissed Fayette on the forehead and left the room.

The chamberlain, who had been waiting to speak with her about Dar, greeted Ysbeth in the hall. Ysbeth was concerned the boy would be a distraction for Fayette. It was clear to her that Fayette had feelings for this boy, and this would not do. She had plans for Fayette's future, and a vagabond from Cornwall did not fit into those plans.

"The boy is in the stockade. We know nothing of him, except that he is a foreigner. What would you have me do with him?" the chamberlain asked.

"He did bring her back to us, we owe him that. We need to find some acceptable way to get rid of him," Ysbeth said. "Leave him where he is for now and bring him to me in the morning. Between now and then, I will decide his fate."

Sharing a cell with a family of mice, Dar had been awake all night, listening to the constant scratching and scurrying. He had just managed to fall asleep when the morning sun peeked through the bars of the small window that overlooked the valley where he had brought Fayette. Had she forgotten him? He wondered if she was in a similar cell in another part of the castle. He got up and walked over to the door. A small barred window was in the center of the small wooden door. Looking out, he could see a guard standing outside in the hall. He called out and asked the guard to come closer.

"Do you know where they took the woman I came in with?" Dar inquired.

"I don't think you should worry about her. You should be more concerned with what will happen when they come for you," the guard said and returned to his post.

"I haven't done anything!" Dar yelled.

"Yeah, that's what they all say! Just pipe down in der," he demanded. It was another hour before the chamberlain came for him. The guard opened the door and drew his sword on him. Frightened of what might come next, Dar jumped back into the cell. A very tall man ducked his head and then entered the cell. He was sickly thin and very old. He placed a hand on the shoulder of the menacing guard to relax his stance.

"There is no need for that. This man is our guest," the tall man said to the guard, who returned his sword to its scabbard. "I am the chamberlain of the duchess. You are Dar LaCross, I presume?"

"Um, yes. I am Dar LaCross of Cornwall," he said without thinking.

"The duchess, Lady Ysbeth, would have a word with you," the tall man said.

"I came in with a woman. What has happened to her?" Dar asked.

"She has been taken care of, and now the duchess would like a word with you," the chamberlain said in an emotionless monotone. "She hasn't done anything. It was all me. What have you done with her?" Dar demanded.

"Calm yourself, sir! Lady Fayette is safe and in her chambers. Would you now follow me to the hall, where the duchess would like to reward you for your service," the chamberlain announced.

Dar wondered if he had heard the man right. "Lady Fayette"? She was just Fayette when he had met her. This certainly explained why she wanted to come directly to the castle instead of stopping in the town to see her family. There was no family in town. He started to wonder who Fayette was and why she did not tell him. He had thought they were friends. He did not know what he had gotten himself into, but whatever it was, he was about to be rewarded for it.

Dar followed the chamberlain to the winding stone stairs, to the courtyard, and to the main hall, where the duchess was waiting. Dar was the son of a nobleman, but he had never been in a great hall and this was the first time he would meet royalty. Once in the hall, the chamberlain beckoned Dar to follow.

"The duchess is eager to meet you, Master LaCross," he said. The duchess was a middle-aged woman, large in stature, who greeted Dar with a smile. She stood up from her chair when he approached with the chamberlain. To show his respect, Dar bowed and kneeled before her, but the duchess touched him on the shoulders and asked him to stand before her.

"It is to you who I owe a debt of gratitude, sir," the duchess said. "Fayette has told me of your journey. Of all the dangers you have faced together. She said that you have saved her life on several occasions."

"This is true, Your Grace," Dar agreed.

"She says that I should reward you for your service to her," the duchess said.

"No, I was happy to bring her home. A reward is not needed. I am just glad that she is safe," Dar said.

"I am very grateful for you bringing her home to us. There must be something that I can grant you. Name it, and it shall be yours," the duchess announced.

"I came to Hibernia to become a knight, but in my journey here, I have come to realize that there are not any knights here," he began to explain.

"Ah, she mentioned this talk of a knighthood. This is some kind of soldier?" the duchess asked.

The chamberlain turned to the duchess and began to explain, "A patron is required, but the boy will need training."

"Ah, Chamberlain, please compose a letter of introduction for our friend, Dar, so that he can join the soldiers at the fort along the border," Ysbeth said. She then returned her gaze to Dar, who seemed unsure of what was happening. "You don't look happy," she said.

"No, Your Grace. I am very pleased. It is what I have wanted. It just seems..." He did not finish his thought. "I am grateful for your generosity, Your Grace," Dar said and then bowed.

"Might I be permitted to see Fayette, er, Lady Fayette one more time to say goodbye?" Dar asked.

"I do not think this wise, Dar LaCross. I will inform her where you have gone. In case she wants to see you," the duchess offered.

Dar took the letter and was given supplies, which he began to strap to the horse stolen from Lemont, the bandit king. Atop the back of the horse appeared the rabbit with his sword. Dar took the sword and put it in his empty scabbard.

"Are those carrots for me?" the rabbit asked.

"Sure, why not," Dar said and handed them to him. The rabbit began chewing on one.

"This *is* what you wanted," the rabbit said.

"Yes, it is," Dar replied and looked into the face of the small animal.

"Then why the long face?" the rabbit asked, but Dar did not answer.

Dar did not know why he did not feel right about what he had been given. With a bit of training, he would become a great knight, he was sure of that.

"These people are crazy. I don't know if I can live here. I might just return home," Dar said while tightening the straps of his gear.

"Aw, come on! If you leave now, you will miss all the good stuff to come," the rabbit pointed out. "You will miss her too. I know you like her."

"She doesn't even know that I exist. She just used me to get home," Dar replied and began to put a harness on the face of the horse.

Meanwhile, the morning sun had been beaming into Fayette's window for hours. She reeled at the thought of seeing Dar and spending the day together with him. For the first time in a very long time, she was excited about something, but she was unsure exactly what it was. As she opened her windows, which overlooked the courtyard, to greet the sun, she looked down to see Dar preparing the horse to leave. A great fear overtook her, and she brought her hand to her face to cover her gaping mouth. Then, without warning, anger overtook and motivated her.

Fayette ran from the window to where Mahj was up and inquiring about what had excited her. Without uttering a word, Fayette ran past Mahj and down the hall. She leaped down several stairs to reach the bottom in record time. The chamberlain had been walking toward the stairs to return to his apartment but stopped when he saw Fayette running for the door in less clothing than was respectable for a young woman. She ran through the door and across the courtyard, where Dar was already leading the horse out toward the gatehouse.

"You're not leaving, are you?" she yelled to him, panting to catch her breath.

Dar stopped and turned toward her, but before he could say anything, she punched him.

"You were just going to leave without saying goodbye," she demanded.

"Lady Ysbeth said I should go to the fort on the borderlands if I am to become a knight," Dar explained.

"Are you serious? Are you on this knight thing again?" she asked.

Fayette looked disappointed that he was leaving her. He was leaving her, and that was the crux of her anger. She bent over, seemingly in pain, but not from running. She felt an overwhelming pain in her heart. Dar stood concerned for her while she paced back and forth. When she stood up to face Dar, her face was wet from tears running down her face.

"You cannot leave, Dar LaCross. You pledged yourself to me, did you not?" Fayette asked.

Dar nodded and agreed. *I did swear to keep her safe and to bring her home, and here she is,* he thought. He was curious where this line of questioning was going to lead him.

"You are in my service to keep me safe, to protect me, and, Dar, I need you," she said, tears running down her neck.

"Yes, but the duchess—"

Fayette did not let him answer. "You are *my* knight. Don't you see that? You are *the* knight of Hibernia! The only one," she said.

The chamberlain reached the door left open by the excited Fayette and hoped to catch her before she did something rash. The duchess did not want her and Dar to be together, and it would seem that his leaving had sparked an unexpected response from her. Reaching the doorway leading to the courtyard, the chamberlain stood helplessly as he watched Dar and Fayette standing in the morning sun, sharing a long embrace. A smile crept across his bony face as he wondered what the future would hold for these two unconventional lovers. In a world where nothing is guaranteed and nothing is given, Dar and Fayette had found their piece of happiness.